בס"ד

for Tosh &

with g

for your w

& friendship.

David

Jerusalem

May 1997

THE STEPMAN

by
David Margolis

THE PERMANENT PRESS
SAG HARBOR, NEW YORK

Library of Congress Cataloging-in-Publication Data

Margolis, David,
The Stepman / David Margolis
p. cm.
ISBN 1-877946-76-1
1. Stepfathers--United States--Fiction 2. Married
People--United States--Fiction. I. Title.
PS3563.A6493S74 1996
813' .54--dc20 95-22755
CIP

First edition, November 1996—1400 copies.

THE PERMANENT PRESS
Noyac Road
Sag Harbor, New York 11963

For my mother
For my father

We poets in our youth begin in gladness,
But thereof come in the end despondency and madness.
—Wordsworth

"If you find a family that's 'blended,' somebody got creamed."
—Family psychologist Patricia Papernow

PART ONE

THE WIFE,
THE JOB,
THE KIDS,
THE HOUSE ON THE HILL

CHAPTER 1

My name is Abner Minsky, a name combining biblical warrior with burlesque king. The great Minsky—the one who could pick the girls—was, as a matter of fact, some sort of remote fourth cousin to us Flatbush Minskys. And of course, since all the Jews are related to one another, even Abner—*the* Abner, King David's general—shares some blood with me. My own growing up, however, though it featured elements of vaudeville, had no conquests or gorgeous girls.

Early in life, however (such may be the power over us of our names), I chose a form of biblical burlesque for my work: I became a poet. That is not an unusual vocation for a Jew, I think, this wanting the tongue to kick up its legs and dance for the sake of God the High.

But poetry is an impractical choice. When we are young, we can live on joy, and the world cooperates to pay us a living for our songs. Not a lot, but I didn't mind being poor then, and there are alternative rewards for the poet: One joins the private brotherhood of unacknowledged legislators of the world; one knows oneself as maven of reality; one impresses certain types of women.

Poets get no honor, however. "Oh, you're a poet," a sociologist friend said once, dismissing an idea of mine, "you live in a fantasy world." Yes, this is an age when sociologists instruct poets. That may itself explain why poets live in a fantasy world. Do you know where sociologists live?

Next door to psychologists.

I know something about psychologists. Right now, in fact, I am sitting in my weekly menage-a-trois with Lora—that's my wife, Lora Sachsman—and our marriage counselor, Mrs. Kramer, a "trained" psychologist. One hour a week, the three of us sit together in a room and analyze selected events. The worst thing about psychologists is that they make you start to think like a psychologist, when what you want to do is think like a poet and not analyze every goddamn little—

Mrs. Kramer is a nice lady, crisp and soft-spoken, a few years younger than us, about thirty-two, pregnant with her first child. She has a serious face and caring brown eyes. In a different situation, I might like her. Here, I don't completely trust her, though she has merited my grudging respect by occasional sturdy insights. I also put up with her because, like many pregnant women, she has trouble keeping her knees together, and my attention is sometimes rewarded with a glimpse of upper thigh.

But I am not watching Mrs. Kramer now. Now I am turned to the other corner of our triangle, faced off with Lora Sachsman. It is much harder for me to describe Lora. Because I see Lora so much, I hardly know what she looks like. On the other hand, I hardly look at her most of the time, because I hate her so much.

But now I have met her eyes across our hypotenuse. I have just finished recounting a happening of last night. While I spoke, Lora was very noticeably restraining herself from violating the ground rule that allows each of us to speak without interruption. Little inarticulate half syllables popped out of her mouth, whole flowers of thought she had to nip in the bud. And she has been just not able to get comfortable in her chair—her legs, her arms, her head—. Yes, she has been a lovely study in exasperation, and my deep esthetic pleasure in this has even moved me to speak more slowly than I normally do, in order to enjoy her distress for a few moments more.

But now I am done at last, and my rough beast, her hour come round at last, readies her response.

This is my wife Lora Sachsman:

Her face is oval. Once it was angelically beautiful to me. Ten years have passed. At thirty-five, her features have thickened, she has gained some weight, her skin has coarsened, and I see her face objectively as rather plain, though it has both charm and "character." Her eyes are large and brown, and she has a very prominent nose, a strong Jewish nose with which she has an ancient love-hate relationship. Her best feature is her mouth, which is richly sensual with a small fish-like curl at the corner of one lip. It is an eater's mouth, with secrets.

Right at this moment, however, Lora's face is neither charming nor even plain and certainly not sensual. It is a gargoyle, hard as stone, the nose beak-like in anger. Her brown hair, which was once long and flowing and colored from sunshine with blonde and auburn highlights, Lora has recently cropped quite close, giving her the demented, slightly abused look of a French collaborator girl—this is a current feminist style, I think—and it stands right now in little upright tufts from Lora tugging at it in her exasperation. She is wearing a man's plaid flannel shirt under baggy purple overalls. Perhaps this is another feminist style, a cross between Paul Bunyan and Bozo the Clown.

Now she is getting ready to speak. Her palms pin her knees, making twin columns of her arms, and she thrusts her face forward. The muscles under her cheeks are grinding with irritation, and soon she will begin to say, in no uncertain tone, exactly what she thinks, precisely where I have gone wrong. I know from long experience, however, that my wife's militant honesty will not necessarily include such small subcategories of truthful discourse as factual accuracy or sticking to the topic; these she regards as forms of oppression, unfair restrictions on her right to free expression. The New Woman don't take no shit from nobody.

To be candid, I am not even certain what we are fighting about this time. Last night she started. I was in Hannah's room, playing with Hannah, our two-year-old. Lora was in the living room, mending Hannah's daycare blanket, or so I thought. Dinner was over; it was a quiet domestic scene. Then I heard her rattling in the kitchen. Then she marched in. "I'd like you to clean up the kitchen," she snapped.

Immediately, like an LSD flashback, I was in it, figuring. The kitchen has three main areas that require maintenance: the sink (with dishes), the countertops, the table. I had cleaned the counters earlier in the evening, after feeding Hannah her dinner. The dishes I'd be damned if I would do: Lora prepares food for herself, then leaves the dishes soaking in old water, in contravention of a clear agreement between us that we wash the dishes from our own snacks. Tonight I knew that, except for two coffee cups of mine and Hannah's bowl, all the dishes in the sink were Lora's—she saves them up for a week, then marches in and demands I do them. (It has a kind of raw logic to it: the dishes are dirty, she wants them cleaned—so who should wash them, Hannah?)

"I don't want to," I said politely.

Lora turned and went out with a face like a brick.

In a moment she was back, with mortar. "I feel you don't cooperate in our life together. It's not like having a husband, it's not even like having a roommate, it's like living with a hostile stranger—"

She stopped and stood there, demanding a response. I decided to cooperate. A soft answer turneth away wrath. A small docility might save me lots of talking later. But I wasn't about to bow down to her idol—there is some s. I will not eat. "I'll do the table, but I won't do the dishes," I told her with earnest civility. "I'm willing to help," I added, "but I don't like being barked at and ordered around."

Unimpressed, she wheeled angrily and went, probably to get her trowel.

Hannah is at the window calling "Yadoo yadoo" to things she sees flying through her head, my sparkling child. I am reclined in her comfy red vinyl beanbag chair, harmlessly hanging out, but I rise and lumber into the kitchen to take care of the table, as offered. But the grim-faced brick-layer is already there, slugging the phone book, the saltshaker and two days of junk mail *onto* the phone table, *onto* the spice shelf, *into* the garbage, her mouth looking as if she has been sucking strained squash through a straw for the last hour.

"I wanted it done right away," she informs me tightly.

Oh. Right away. Chop chop.

And do you know why? "Phyllis called and said she'd drop by and I don't want the kitchen looking like a wreck." Get it?—for the sake of her friend Phyllis. This is the stuff on which saints build whole careers; I should be grateful for the opportunities for spiritual advancement my wife offers me at every moment.

After Phyllis left (it was a good visit, I think, they analyzed their lives for a couple of hours and came out of the bedroom looking sweaty but relaxed, like ping-pong champions after a workout)—after Phyllis left, Lora and I sat in the living room. Hannah was asleep (I had put her to bed), the house was quiet. I was reading, Lora was sewing. Time to wind up and move toward bed ourselves. Lora said, "I don't feel like we spend any time together."

La bouche dropped open and a bilious tone dribbled out in words. "What are you talking about? What are we doing right now?"

"I feel like you don't want to spend time with me—to really be with me."

"Well," I said, all saintliness departed, "shall we look at the record?" I ticked off the days on my fingers: Thursday, a movie and out for a drink afterward; Friday afternoon, working together cleaning our apartment; Friday evening, together with friends; Saturday morning, home together; Saturday afternoon, shopping together; Sunday brunch together and a late afternoon picnic with friends; lunch together on Monday, just the two of us; last night separate activities, yes, and then this evening you pick a fight with me. What is the *matter*?

"I don't consider it quality time," she said, ticking her fingers back at me: no real companionship, too much time with friends, constant interruptions from Hannah, not being really together. "And a lot of Saturday morning I stayed in our room reading," she fingered at me finally, as if I had forced her in there to the lonely solace of her books.

I shrugged. I thought it was an okay week, as nice as a week with Lora can be, the fruit of my constant vigilance to get into no situation that might cause a fight. An exhausting vigilance, that, but I truly thought these last few days had been okay, better than the week before at least, with no ambushes, train wrecks, epidemics, or terrorist massacres; nicely contained. We passed for normal.

"You never want to be with me," she went on, relentless. "You never show me any affection."

"I never show—." I stop, imagining I will be able to calm myself, discuss this first with my inner heart, then provide an answer that will ease us out of our stalemate. Stale mate.

But I am fooling myself. I am too thin-skinned after these years of friction: touch me and I bleed, it all comes leaking out. "You are a goddamn porcupine, do you know that?" I inquire. "You present your sharp quills and then beg to be embraced." My voice becomes almost languid to my own ear, merely descriptive. I am not even angry as I say, "Why don't you just leave me alone?"

Lora is sitting in the armchair, looking down at her lap, her face a study in darkness as she stirs her own deep concoction of anger and grief, confusion and guilt. And love—yes, love is mixed up somewhere in this too, deeply mixed in.

She does not speak, she does not look at me. Finally she gets up and walks past me into the bedroom and shuts the door. I do not look at her or call to her as she goes.

Where are we now? What is happening to us now and what will happen next? Should I follow her, apologize—apologize for what?—and try to make it be all right? To leave it at this deadness I know will lead to new torments tomorrow. It would be politic to say something to her—Lora likes that. Lora will appreciate that. Otherwise, we'll be not-talking-to-each-other, and then we'll have to have a fight to break through it, or some sort of sodden emotional scene, thicker with misery the longer I wait, as I know from deadly experience. So yes, I agree with the voice of my best self, I should rise and knock, speak and comfort; I am moved to do it, almost.

I do not do it. I sit in my chair, enjoying the simplicity of solitude and silence, the small animal comforts left to me, postponing anything else. It is the familiar living room of my home, with its off-white walls, its shelves of books, its second-hand sofa and chairs with pictures—Lora's paintings—hanging above them, and I feel in it like a stranger, playing for my own grim pleasure the tape loops of my unhappiness, drinking the bitter elixir of my disappointment and somehow finding comfort in it. It is my heart, and I eat it because it is bitter and because it is my heart. Yes, and because no one can take it away from me.

After imbibing the dregs of this dark wine, I must have fallen asleep sitting up, for when I wake the lights are on and I feel drunk, hung over. It is 2 a.m. and the house is still. I stumble to the bathroom, then to the bedroom. Lora has not left the light on for me, which I know means, according to our code, that I am shit-deep in trouble.

But I don't mind; silence and darkness are my friends.

So I climb into the marriage bed and sleep along one edge, taking care neither to touch nor to disturb in any way my sleeping wife.

I wish on all my enemies a love affair like this.

CHAPTER 2

When I recount this story to Mrs. Kramer, including but not primarily addressing Lora, I half hope to convince or cajole Mrs. Kramer into seeing that I am right. I want to compel her to break through her professional veneer for once and say the honest truth: that Lora acts like a hysterical teenage girl. The extent of Mrs. Kramer's responses, however, amount to allowing occasional small furrows of interest, concern, regret and possibly horror to pass across her features. She does not vote. When I am done, she nods and says, "Uh huh," then asks Lora to speak.

So now Lora comes up to bat and tells a story that is basically the same as mine but utterly different. In Lora's version, she came into Hannah's room and asked me—asked me! She has the gall to say it and, worse, the gall apparently to believe it—if I would help her straighten up the kitchen, but I flatly refused (refused!), as if I think she is supposed to be my servant. He ignores our previous agreement, she says, under which he has the obligation, if he prepares a meal for Hannah, to clean up after it—not merely *swab* the counters, she says in her best bitch tone, but wash the utensils and clear the table as well.

Now it is my turn to stop myself from interrupting. The dishes in the sink were, most of them, hers. I know it, but I cannot prove it; it is a classic case of my word against hers. And yet it is true, *her* dishes were in the sink—

My God, we are arguing over whose dishes are in the sink. This is how debased we have become. This is what the poet is reduced to. Violence would be nobler.

Lora is really warming up now, spewing details and accusations, but I have flown away. I am alone on a promontory overlooking the sea, far from the humiliation of disputing over who should wash a few dirty dishes. An ancient king wearing the bleak crown of humanity, I feel a familiar, almost pleasurable despair drop over my shoulders. Somewhere so far away that the sound of it is slightly disassociated from the moving of her lips, as music is from a seat in the upper reaches of the amphitheater, I can still hear Lora kvetching. Now she is accusing me of coldness, of refusing to respond when she brings up, as she did last night, such serious issues as my unwillingness to spend quality time with her (quality time, I remember dreamily, is a phrase generally used to describe child care).

She reproaches me for my continual dissatisfaction with everything—with her, with our family, with my job, with my life; for being grumpy and grim-faced all the time; for sarcasm; for failing to listen to her when she speaks; for greeting her enthusiasms with a look that stares past her; for not acting as if I care; for not caring; for not touching; for not making her feel loved. All my love, she complains, I give to Hannah; Hannah I cuddle with and coo to, Hannah I hold and confide in, Hannah I will take time out for, will go out of my way for. But with her, says my wife to our arbiter, with her I refuse to go anywhere. I never even want to go out of the house, let alone invite her to a movie or to dinner, and never never never, she says, do I ever say, "I love you," her voice breaking, "He never tells me he loves me any more."

I sit there in a kind of panic, afraid that one of them will have the common sense to ask me, "Well, Abner, do you love her?" But neither of them does, and I am saved from having to face or confess the truth.

Instead, I sit quietly in this small motel-like chamber, with its plain carpeting and unobtrusive paneled walls and its three sensible chairs, and I listen to Lora Sachsman weep. And somehow my eyes too have become wet. Nothing has changed for me, nothing any longer changes anything for me, but I am not quite a block of stone: I feel so much deep regret, so much disappointment, so much sorrow for myself and for Lora too, because we both wanted, expected, deserved something more than this terrible crippled limping together in harness that we do, this pulling ourselves apart, this having nothing. I forgive nothing, only I know in this moment of grief how much we have lost.

Mrs. Kramer's face is filled with our reflected sorrow; her expression encourages us to feel our pain while she sits silent, letting us stew in our steamy juices. My throat burns with the effort to hold back sound and feeling. Lora sobs and sniffles to herself and finally takes a tissue out of the box that is considerately placed on the table between us. We are not the first people to use tissues out of this box, here in the self-confrontation factory.

But it is all so useless. The first time around it had productive possibilities, perhaps. Two years ago when we came to another agency, a different professional, with the same stories, he gave us exercises to do: make dates with one another, make clear agreements, begin to rebuild the trust. That was his phrase: "Begin to rebuild the trust." "Let's see if we can rebuild the trust." "The both of you are such nice people, you just need to rebuild the trust."

Now here we are again, needing to rebuild the trust we never rebuilt the first time. After a while, you stop believing in the possibility of improvement. After a while, trust becomes a secondary issue. After a while, you just want a little peace and quiet. I think I could live without agreements, I could even live without love, I think I could put up with everything, if she would just leave me alone.

Lora's face has softened now. She has relaxed into her chair, no longer Super Feminist Attacking the Forces of Male Ego. This is the vulnerable Lora, the Lora who pleads for help—the Entrapping Lora instead of the Attacking Lora.

Ten years now, ten years we have been together. For other people, we are a landmark, a lighthouse—such bright people, such talented, interesting people, such a nice, creative family, how good it is to see people working hard at making it work and succeeding. Some days it seems we owe it to others to stay together—owe it to our parents, owe it to our friends, owe it to all the years we have been together, to the children, to all the promises we made in the beginning to cherish and protect each other, to love forever, to work it out no matter what.

Yes, many cords of responsibility are knotted into this knot.

But now our time is up, Mrs. Kramer tells us softly, bringing us back from the silent recollections in which we are separately lost. She begins her weekly summation. A part of your difficulty, she explains to us in her modulated voice, is that the privacy that you, Abner, need from Lora taps into her deep fear of being abandoned; while the comfort and loving engagement that you need, Lora, arouses Abner's deep fear of being smothered and swallowed up.

"We're perfectly matched," says Lora, winning a measured smile from Mrs. Kramer.

"Perhaps you are. But if you are to stay together, you must find ways to both let each other alone and be willing to fully engage with each other."

This is the poetry of the psychologists: the poetry of irrelevant truths.

And then we are out in the street together, walking side by

side but not touching or looking at each other—perfectly matched. Dinnertime is approaching, evening is quickening faintly in the streets of Athens, New York, and the streets are thickened with traffic for our town's brief rush hour. On the sidewalks, housewives with children, lawyers with attaché cases, students from the college all hurry, hurry into their evenings.

As Lora and I walk, I am aware of her as a dark shape beside me, a kind of blinder were I to glance that way, while on my other side I may regard freely the pleasant, open street and my fellow townspeople, strangers with unknowable private lives of their own.

It is springtime, warm and fragrant. The coeds are blooming, the young mothers are fully ripened, the lawyers have the money and the freedom to do whatever they want to do. And I, Abner Minsky, am trapped.

Lora and I need to pick up Hannah at day care and go home to prepare dinner. My preference would be to do one of these things while Lora does the other, but I know that Lora will be angry if I suggest it. She will feed it to the fire of her anger that I avoid spending time with her, avoid being a normal family with her. And she is right: I would rather be alone, with no guard up, than constantly have to consider if what I want to do is going to cause a fight between us.

"Shall we go get Hannah together?" Lora asks at the corner.

"Sure," I agree. Discretion is my only choice, valor—forget it. I am used to such small self-restrictions in the cause of peace, and Hannah is delighted to have us come together to get her. We put her in her stroller and trudge home in the slanted late-afternoon light, another one of those young families on their way to dinner, passing for normal.

Both Lora and I know, however, that this is only a brief interlude between crises. We began our session with Mrs. Kramer by mentioning it, then got deflected: Tonight, the kids—Lora's children from her first marriage and my stepchildren for the last ten years: Eli, fifteen, and Ella, thirteen—return from a spring-break visit to their father and stepmother in West Virginia.

I am not looking forward to it one bit.

CHAPTER 3

After our visits to Mrs. Kramer, Lora and I usually get along a little better for a while. Although certain sore wounds have been rubbed raw all over again, we have both bled some and we remember each other as worthy adversaries and former friends. We have some small compassion for one another, and it even occurs to us to forgive, if not forget, although we are unable to do either.

So the evening went well, pretty much as scheduled, which is as well as can be expected. We cooperated to prepare dinner for the three of us: Quiet and efficient, I cooked omelettes while Lora made salad, toasted bread and set the table. Our plump Hannah, always ready for another meal, pulled herself onto her hind legs and tried to climb into her high chair, and Lora hoisted her up and gave her a carrot to practice gnawing on.

Over dinner, we tended to pay attention to Hannah rather than each other and conversed on safe subjects. I, an instructor of writing at Athens College, brought Lora up to date in the ongoing dramas of several students and colleagues. She, a part-time job counselor for adolescents at the Athens Alternative Community Counseling Center (A-C3, in the local lingo), kindly betrayed confidences to me about her clients, in order to keep the conversation going.

So gossip gets us through dinner. But by 7:30, my wife and I are fighting again. The kids are coming in at the bus station in a short while, and Lora wants me to go with her to get them. "I'd rather stay home and write in my journal," I tell her.

This sets her off, for she is very sensitive to any slight from me toward her children, and soon (though we have discussed it no further) she has made herself so furious she can barely speak. For Lora, that is very angry indeed.

In between little squirts and squelches of pure sound, she gives me a piece of her mind: "They're your stepchildren. Don't pretend they aren't anything to you. You raised them. You chose to be their father. You made them trust you and told them they could count on you. Now you decide to pull out. Even if you're angry with me, you don't have to take it out on them. It isn't their fault." Two beats, a shifting of gears. "They love you. You're very important to them. Why do you want to cut yourself off from them like this, as if they don't mean anything to you?"

She is able to go on like this for a very long time. It would take me a half hour to think up even half a sentence of response, all my feelings still dammed up behind my eyes, threatening to leak out. But I won't allow that. It all boils down to this: I will not cry and I will not do what you want me to do. And that, at last, holding on to simple identity, is what I figure out to say. "I don't want to go to the bus station, Lora, and I'm not going to go."

I am sponging crumbs off the counter and Lora is cleaning dinner off Hannah. We both pay sharp attention to our small chores. Hannah, who does want to go meet Eli and Ella at the bus station, plays with blobs of applesauce that remain on her tray while Lora works on her face. A sponge in one hand, crumbs in the other, I turn to Lora and coolly offer a compromise. "If it's really important to you, I'm willing to go. But since I'll be giving up writing time, I want you to give me back that time tomorrow evening by being in charge of Hannah for an extra hour or so."

Lora's mouth opens and closes like a fish, she is so mad. She turns and takes three short steps toward me. Her eyes are so angry that I feel a short surge of apprehension: Will she rush for a kitchen knife and stab me? Harm herself or Hannah? Scream so loud the neighbors will call the police? Have a fit and need to be taken to the hospital? The kids are due in on the bus in half an hour. Have I finally gone too far?

But she gets hold of herself, and in a quiet, deadly voice she says into my face, "Fuck you." She is in cold control now. "You'll pay for this, Abner," she warns me. I experience a second thrill of anticipation. She is preparing her revenge. I may have won this time, but she is already planning the rematch, unimaginable acts of emotional vandalism are being vouchsafed to me in this moment.

How unpleasant this woman is, I think to myself. She is still wearing her baggy purple overalls, and her face is close enough for me to see her pores. I used to find her beautiful.

"Here you go again," I say cordially. "You have the notion that it is somehow an obligation of mine to go with you to meet your kids at the bus depot. And you don't even leave open to me the possibility of not going; it has to be a big fight for me not to go. Even if I were their father, I might not want to go." I am being reasonable now. "It doesn't have to be a big fight between you and me. I'm not rejecting them by not going to the bus station with you—you're making it be something it's not. I mean," I add, playing trump, "didn't I make soup this afternoon because I knew they were coming home tonight?"

Yes, it's true. In a small spirit of nostalgia for the kids, this afternoon, before our appointment with Mrs. Kramer, I prepared a quick tomato-vegetable soup now burbling on low heat in the crock-pot on the counter behind me. To the onions, carrots and two potatoes, the canned tomatoes and corn kernels, I am planning to add at the last minute a small package of alphabet noodles, which I know the children love. I am not a bad guy.

I can see Lora's face soften as she begins to doubt herself, to wonder if in fact she has misjudged all this. Is she, I can almost hear her think, operating out of a purely internal drama, as I have many times suggested? The crock of soup has warmed her, awakened the possibilities of gratitude. I have almost won.

I press home with a simple truth. "You know," I say in my most caring, social worker tone, imitating Mrs. Kramer, "it has to be true that Eli and Ella are more important, more essential, more central to your life than to mine—after all, you're their mother. And you have to be willing to give me some space to determine my own relationship with them, now that they're adolescents and don't require all that body care any more, the way they did when they were little. You have to allow me and them to find out by ourselves what relationship we're going to have now."

Since Mrs. Kramer has said similar things, I know that Lora will hear me. Yes, the flush of madness has faded from her cheeks and her eyes look partially inward now. She nods finally, surrendering to my superior logic. "Okay," she says (but her teeth are still clenched, by which I know that I will indeed pay for this in the end), "do whatever you want to do. Come or don't come." She means it for this moment and turns back to Hannah, who has smeared the applesauce all over her face again while glancing worriedly back and forth between her mother and father.

"Oh, shit," says Lora and starts to clean her up again.

"Oh s'it," says Hannah, learning her mother's ways.

"Look," I say to Lora's back, still being Mr. Reasonable, "I'll do whatever you want me to. If it's so important to you, I'll come to the bus station with you. But I want to *arrange* it with you, that's all." (This is shorthand for, I want to cut a deal;

I am pursuing the conversation in order to prove something to myself.)

Calmed enough to think, Lora considers it as she works on Hannah, then tells me that's okay, I should stay home after all. Yes, I was right, and we have now come to the hub and the nub of it, though a healthy learned respect for self-preservation restrains me from speaking it aloud: Confronted with a clear opportunity, my wife does not (and never will, I would say) choose to return anything to me for what I give to her kids. She would rather I not go to greet them, which was only a few moments ago the issue of the century, than that she should have to offer any small reward, any gesture in return.

Fine with me, sweetheart. And so I go into my small study and sit down at my desk and write it all down in my secret notebook, dreading the inevitable moment when my stepchildren are going to walk through the door and everything will start being the way it is—and I will start being the way I am—when they're around.

CHAPTER 4

The time before they come is ten years long.

Ten years ago, age twenty-five, I stored everything I cared to keep in my parents' garage in Brooklyn, sold my Lower East Side railroad flat to the next sucker in line and stuck my thumb out like a mailbox, posting myself to California, the land of gold, doing the immigrant shtick like Minskys from a former time.

In those days, the afterspill of the Sixties, people were still friendly; half of them had a joint already rolled. I saw the swift macadam from the cabs of sixteen-wheelers and through the windshields of a lot of VW vans. Even the boredom of the wandering made a kind of heavenly music as the intercontinental highway hummed and lugged through Pennsylvania, Illinois, the Plains. . . .

As I traveled, I knew myself the beneficiary of many chance encounters legislated elsewhere, for purposes I did not need to know, and wrote down in my book all the levels of reality it was my poet's gift to see.

Out there on the road, I was happy and self-sufficient. Protected by Cyna my Muse, the personal goddess of my private mind, I allowed the road to bear me where I wanted it to go, another Johnny Appleseed sowing poetry in the soil of every random collision. Poet as Primal Man, Poet as Witness, Poet as Priest, Poet as Blank Sheet of Paper (did someone whisper Foolscap?).

Once, on the high plateau called Dakota, I stood beneath a cloud so close I could leap up and touch its filmy stuff. Yes, my head was in the clouds! I touched the sky! Dakota, Wyoming, Utah . . . I was happy. Praise God for the monumental ribbon of the Interstate!

And what made my wandering perfect was that I had a destination. I was headed for Mars, and Mars knew I was on my way.

Mars was Marshall Silverman, a change of name that indicates how great a distance a boy born and bred in Brooklyn may travel. Mars was my oldest friend, my best friend, my favorite wildman. In high school—to give one example of his greatness—he had locked the faculty advisor of the school paper in the "morgue" as a protest against censorship. "I put him in with all past issues," he told the Principal and only barely escaped expulsion. In college, that high school for grownups, he also had other plans. "We'll go to Oregon," he urged me, "we'll go to India. How can you stand this?"

But I wouldn't go, and he finally sailed west one day on his own. Several months later I got a picture postcard of the Golden Gate Bridge in its splendor and a message that haunted me while I dutifully completed my degree: "If it isn't perfect it's no good," he wrote. "Come on."

But I stayed. I got the degree and then I got an editorial job. I wrote poems for escape, doing mind-travel. It took a broken heart, the woman-I-loved in another's arms entwined, to make living in New York feel like a form of pursuing death; but worse: Death is a natural function, whereas digging your own grave is weird.

So, pulling the plug on all the deadly virtues, I had pushed off at last without a plan. It was my twenty-fifth year to heaven, and when I touched down at last like Noah's dove on Mars's hillside one eventide late in the summer of 1974, he was there in yellow porch light, waiting for me: Mars, my red planet, his bearded face as wreathed in smiles to see me as my clean-shaven one was for him, and our arms went around each other in manly greeting, true to the pledge we had made long ago to be friends and brothers and to begin again simply wherever we had left off the time before, eternal enemies of time and distance.

It was good to see him.

After we hugged and yowled and laughed, Mars brought me inside his house. And that was the night, a free and happy man, that I first met Lora Sachsman Rosen.

Mars's house was like a leftover stage-set from the Sixties: slightly run-down, decorated in a confusion of threadbare and colorful styles, crowded with people, noisy and disorganized. I loved it immediately as an artifact of my new life.

Mars dropped my backpack into a corner in the general mess and introduced me to Rabbit, the compact, dark-haired girl who was his current love. "How was your trip?" she asked.

"I don't want to know about your trip, man," Mars interrupted. "Tomorrow, I'll debrief you, you'll debrief me, we'll start to act as if you just got here." Rabbit made a face at him, but he was already settled down rolling a doobie as big around as the smaller moon of the fourth planet. "Tonight, man, you just walked over with Rabbit from Potrero Hill for the evening, we're gonna get stoned and practice flying, okay?"

Okay? I'm here. I have arrived. I have made it across prairie and mountain to Land's End. My face has been abused by wind for two weeks straight, my jeans are soggy with sweat and dirt, I am unbathed in the extreme, I have carried my pack 3,000 miles, and all the muscles in my legs and back are biting me hard. Yes, okay—light the joint.

He did, I got stoned to the gills and swam into the scene.

There was a lot of energy compressed into that house. Aside from Mars and Rabbit, beaming at me wherever I went, there were Lance and Nancy, a blond look-alike couple, cooking an organic vegetarian feast because it was Al's last night. And Al and Lora Rosen and their kids, Eli and Ella, who were seven and four years old then, were having their family breakup.

Al had kinky hair, a wiry beard and manic bright-blue eyes. He was leaving the next morning for British Columbia to live in an ashram and study with a lady swami. That explained his eyes. Right now he was camped out in the living room among piles of his possessions, filling boxes with books, tools, clothing and what I would have called junk—machine and engine components, plumbing valves, parts of things—preparatory to storing the boxes in sheds behind the house. Meanwhile, his kids were climbing all over him, trying for last-minute goodies of attention.

A long line of his stuff, arranged in small piles like decorative stones along a path, extended behind him and down the narrow corridor onto which the bedrooms opened. For some reason, instead of taking the cardboard boxes into the bedroom to fill, he had brought everything he owned out into public space, making his packing a public event.

At the big dining table, watching him, sat Lora, his wife. Introduced, I nodded a greeting, routinely cataloguing her: thin, sharp-featured face, braided rope of brown hair, wide, dark eyes—the Jewish Indian-princess look, and pleasantly heavy in the chest and hips. The little girl, Ella, had her mother's dark eyes, and the boy had his father's blue ones. Both kids were talking in high whines, pleading with Al to send them things, demanding gifts from among the objects Al was packing, asking if they could come to visit him soon at the ashram, running back to Mommy at the table to make sure she still was there.

Mommy had in front of her a bag of cashews which she was eating in a mechanical holding-on-for-dear-life way, while rolling her eyes elaborately at Mars and Rabbit about some of the things her husband was saying to their kids ("Sure, you can come and spend the whole summer with me," "Sure, I'll send you anything you want"). I understood that Al was departing in an open-ended way and leaving the wife and kids, but I was by then very stoned, which made everything seem, if not necessarily normal, then at least perfect in itself and therefore fully entertaining. I was having a good time, glad that it wasn't me who had to be going anywhere right now or was getting left behind.

Meanwhile, I learned why Rabbit's name was Rabbit; because she must say Rabbit, Rabbit as soon as she wakes each morning in order to avoid certain unpleasant consequences which she does not name. She follows this intelligence with a little well-practiced soft-shoe routine with Mars, the two of them perfectly in synch on the two-step and singing harmony together on "Tea for Two." In my preliminary judgement, they seem happy, easily intimate and having fun.

I wander into the kitchen to investigate Lance and Nancy, while Rabbit puts Crosby, Stills and Nash on the player, setting a tone.

You who are on the road
must have a code
that you can live by. . . .

In the kitchen, Nancy is supervising a cauldron of brown rice steaming on the stove while she chops vegetables for Lance to sauté on another burner. While Lance drops green peppers off the cutting board into a wok, Nancy mashes tofu in a bowl for mock-cheese pie.

Why mock? To avoid milk products, Lance explains, and because tofu is healthier than cheese—more protein, less fat, fewer calories, less processed—. Yes, I am in California!

Nancy is glad to inform me that they are hoping soon to move back to communal land up north from which they had moved to San Francisco, forced into city trips by the need to earn money. We are getting along nicely when suddenly over the sound of the music and the clattering of kitchen utensils come the shrill shrieks of small children being murdered.

I poke my head around the doorpost to spy it out: Al has given something to Ella but not to Eli, I report back to the kitchen. Nancy heaves a heavy sigh. "It'll be hard on her and the kids, but I'm glad he's leaving."

"How come?" I oblige.

"They're hard people to live with," Nancy explains. "I would say it to their faces, too."

"You have," Lance reminds her.

"That's right, I have." She warms to the topic. "He brings junk home from all over town and lets it accumulate all over the house and all over the yard until you can hardly move. And she's generally talking about a thousand miles an hour about a hundred different things—"

"Unless she's 'depressed,'" Lance says, making it sound like a foreign word. (I'm a New Yorker, so I recognize the dialect.)

"And the kids completely run them," Nancy goes on, folding honey into the tofu mash. I have stumbled into thick politics here.

"They're very nice people," Lance assures me. "They really are, and Al will go miles out of his way for you. It's just that they're so, I don't know—"

"Hard to live with." Nancy and I finish his sentence at the same time, which leaves us all smiling at each other as if we have reached a new level of mutual understanding. I like Lance and Nancy, even if they are unstoned, vegetarian, Protestant, and too thin, with hair so blond it makes the tops of their heads seem slightly out of focus. I like them for being themselves and not having a moment of doubt that that is good enough. Cyna and I both like them for thinking they have nothing to hide, since people who think they have nothing to hide easily reveal the secrets on which poetry thrives. I like them for being kind of dumb, and I am looking forward to the mock-cheese pie.

Wandering back into the living room, I experience a happy surprise to see Mars, whose presence I am not used to yet. He has Rabbit on his lap, and they look surprised to see me, too.

Over at the table, Eli—"Mommy, Mommy, look what Daddy gave me!"—is being ecstatic over a broken pocket calculator with which Al is trying to even the account between him and his sister. Ella is beginning to object, Lora is rolling her eyes and eating cashews, dishes are clanking in the kitchen,

Mars and Rabbit are in their happy world, and the last smoke of the joint is still hovering like a blessing near the ceiling.

When the kids follow Al into the bedroom in the hope of more loot, I sit down in comradely fashion beside Lora. She greets me by offering me some cashews. Keeping her company, I take a few and thoughtfully chew them into cashew butter one at a time, providing sympathetic eye contact and staying helpfully silent, because when I look closely at her face I understand that it is shimmery with her life falling apart around her, that she is holding herself together with some effort and that if I, who am on the road, have any sort of code at all, I ought to try my best to be quietly supportive, neither indifferent nor intrusive.

On the couch, Mars and Rabbit are now playing a bouncing game; Lance and Nancy, bustling back and forth, are stacking plates and silverware on the table beside me, preparatory to the meal; Al has gone to the back of the house to continue packing. In my stoned way, I begin to think that I am the only person here—a stranger, no less—who realizes that this woman is in deep distress.

Something in her vulnerability and need, in the wild-eyed, slightly comic way she keeps eating cashews, is appealing to me. I have already learned that she is an artist and used to live, like me, on the Lower East Side. I like her looks.

So I sit beside her, helping her eat cashews out of a plastic baggie while I make the stoned assessment that the best thing just might be some mundane small talk. I carefully choose questions: "Will you and your kids keep living here?" "What's the lady swami like?" "Do your kids go to school yet?"

She tells me the answers: "That's all I need, to have to move somewhere else," "She wears a turban and goes around doing miracles," and, with a look of horror, "*No, thanks.*" Her thick New York caw soothes me, and I am flattered that she is willing to talk with me. In fact, she is just beginning to explain to me why she will never allow her children to go to public school when somewhere down the corridor Ella, the little girl, loses it completely again and emitting staccato high-pitched screams of alarm bursts into the living room and throws herself onto her mother, landing half in her lap and half on her shoulder.

Lora wraps her arms around the girl and rocks her back and forth making small soothing animal sounds and crooning, "Yes, yes, you're upset, I know, you're worried," only slightly muffling Ella's painful cries. Lance and Nancy appear in the doorway, Rabbit and Mars separate and sit up straight. Ella is the center of attention—mother and child. Her father Al lumbers in from the bedroom with Eli behind him, and no one knows what it's about, except that the immediate cause of Ella's sobbing is not likely to be the real cause.

Al, looking guilty and worried, stands helplessly beside his wife and daughter, letting his hand drift down onto Ella's head. They're a little family tableau, I think poetically, taking another handful of nuts while I watch them with my outsider's deep sympathy, and Lora turns to me, grabs the plastic bag and says sharply, "Don't eat all the fucking cashews, all right?"

I feel like I have been slapped, that is how surprised I am. I realize that I am completely out of place in this tableau, someone caught accidentally in the snapshot. What am I doing here? Why am I sitting here and pretending to be old friends with this woman while her husband is abandoning her and her children are screaming?

I move away, and for the rest of the evening I barely speak to her. On one level, I am completely understanding. These people are in crisis, one must suspend one's normal expectations. Nonetheless, I feel embarrassed and insulted, my callow foolishness revealed, the gift of my good intentions thrown back in my face.

That first meeting is a story Lora and I have told many times over the years since then, to each other and to others. Each of us has different details we find important, and both of us over the years have changed the emphasis of the story, depending on what point we wanted to make ("You can never tell from first meetings." "Even our first encounter showed there was something fiery and deep between us." "From the beginning we had a tendency to misunderstand each other." "Right away I was involved in Lora's family life." "There was something I liked about his face"— "Yeah, that's why you wanted to bite it off . . . .")

But only because of the subsequent journeying does this first scene carry any weight. Only history gives our first argument significance.

In those days, I cared nothing for history: I loved only the here-and-now, with its dangers and promise, willing the shimmering present moment to exist without the dense baggage of the past.

Was that itself my essential mistake, my tragic flaw?

That night I only knew that I had made it to Mars. Breathing the exhilarating air of the Ocean and the Bay, I was at my new beginning.

Always, says Cyna, look in the beginning for the parable of the end.

CHAPTER 5

Now here I am in my little room in Athens, New York. This is the small refuge we have agreed is mine, to which I may close the door and be alone without fear of intrusion. That is what we agreed.

Nonetheless, since Lora has on a number of occasions felt that her emotional state—her awful *need* to work things out and to be reassured—transcended both my need to be still and our agreement, I have screwed a hook and eye into the molding and made it my habit to lock myself in. I do not know what I will do when, refused entrance by a physical barrier, Lora-in-Need will begin to scream and pound against the wood—but I think I will simply continue to sit here at my desk and to cultivate within me scrupulously the inimitable, which is loneliness. That is, wait till it blows over.

Though no one is at home now, I latch the door.

Then I open the closet and wheel myself over in my wooden swivel chair and sit for a while simply watching myself in the mirror attached inside the closet door, trying to figure out how that bearded man, the beginnings of permanent lines settling into the corners of his eyes, reached this cramped present space from expansive beginnings ten years ago. I know that face, it is someone I can talk to, so I lean in conversationally and say aloud, "Abner, old partner, how did we get here? It isn't what we expected ten years ago when we made the choice for freedom and romance, is it?"

And in the glass I shake my head. "No, friend, ten years and forty pounds ago, we didn't know the path would lead us here."

This mirror has seen many things. It has shown me to myself while I masturbated, making of the auto-tickle an auto-esthetic experience as well. From time to time I strip completely naked before it, mainly to embarrass myself. I even have an uncompleted poem—I have not finished a poem in many months—about my relationship with my mirror, called "Hangover:"

> Substantial, prosperous, Abner's belly
> hangs over. Is he a rich man?

From there the poem was to give a guided tour of those forty extra pounds, thick and sticking out their fleshy tongues and refusing to move, as if I have become a bag lady carrying everything I own around with me. Look: a man with breasts. Not large ones, but not firm ones, either—the sorry tits of a fat man, nippling to a point when I lean over. Fleshy fat man's flanks and belly bulges dangling down-O. My cock, not wanting to see the sorry sight, retreats into itself, and if I fold my thighs over, I can hide my sex and be unmanned entirely, a fat-woman sack filled up with shame, anger, self-disgust and food.

A portrait of the artist as a college teacher.

And yet the face in the mirror is mine, my old familiar knowing face, my friend. "Take care of yourself, *viejo*," it tells me softly as I close the closet door and pedal, fully clothed, in my chair on wheels back across the planks to my desk.

My desk is another friend. Poems have been born on this swart slab. Cigarettes and joints have burned memorable dark comet tails into the wood; it is stained with coffee rings and dabs of white-out and scratched by paper clips and the pushing around of my dear old typewriter, another buddy of my bosom.

Yes, in this room I have friends, I have family, and sometimes it is no hardship at all but the greatest grace and joy to sit alone among them in the quiet company of a bookshelf with my favorite volumes, my materials arranged, my notebook ready.

I could be happy in this room forever, I think, if they would send in food.

Can this be me now, the poet and sweet singer? The gift of poesy gone, my project these days is to reread my journals. I may find clues there. Perhaps if I can remember and retell to myself the ecstasy and depth of falling in love with Lora Sachsman, that might be some small redemption. But what lodges in the mind instead is that poor beginning, with cashews. Is the poet destined to eat filth forever? Have I lost sight for always of the Beautiful Face?

Feel sorry for yourself, Abner Minksy, no doubt that will be productive.

I was happy in San Francisco. Mars had his own moving-and-hauling business, *Moving with Mars*, and signed me on for half a day of hard shlepping. It was great: hanging out with my best friend, putting on muscles, learning the city, earning my bowl of rice a day.

And what a city San Francisco is! You turn a corner and there suddenly are the blue waters of the Bay, the Bridge, the cliffs across the Golden Gate, tiny manned ships sailing in the vast waters like details in a painting by Brueghel. It is a city whose inhabitants cultivate flowers in its street dividers, keep it clean, praise it and proudly proclaim their own their mad idiosyncrasies: Hare Krishna women with babies on their saffron hips, young professionals with hippie mustaches, true hippies still holding up the frayed banner of peace, computer geniuses with green skin and dexedrine eyes, tough bikers, flashy gays, cowboys—drummers to every beat. To a Brooklyn boy, the city seemed a country carnival, the very life for which I had inarticulately yearned in dour New York.

I worked for half a day and wandered with my notebook for the second half, writing poems, then found the way home to dinner at my friend's house on the hill, my bluejeans hanging coolly on my hips.

Doors opened for me before I reached them, as if the electronic Eye really was watching. Just when I had begun to hunt for my own place to live, not wanting to spend my life on Mars's living room couch, Lance and Nancy announced their decision to move back up to Chico. "San Francisco," Nancy explained one evening over vegetables, "is just too urban."

I knew they were also frustrated by Mars, the world's most tolerant person, who was glad to eat organic carrots as long as he could wash them down with a Coca-Cola and finish them off with a package of Twinkies. This idea of including all the gods happily together in the same pantheon drove Lance and Nancy into fits.

Meanwhile, Mars, a confirmed city boy, couldn't understand moving to the country. Having an empty lot next door and sheds behind the house with blackberry vines growing on them was as countrified as he was willing to get. "What are you going to do ten miles outside of *Chico*?" he asked.

"Well," said Lance, chewing rhythmically, "we'll garden. We might try to grow a crop to sell commercially. We'll raise chickens and goats. We might be able to sell firewood off part of the land. We—"

"No, no," Mars interrupted him, sounding worried. "I mean what'll you *do*?"

Lance stared at him in perfect noncomprehension.

"He means what'll you do when you want a Twinkie," Lora explained.

That brought a laugh. Meanwhile, a bedroom had become

available. Thus I became a full-fledged member of Mars's little commune.

Which is how the Flow takes care of us, O ye of little faith.

In the couple of weeks it took Lance and Nancy to make their getaway, Nancy made me her special confidant. She had, it turned out, a lot of negative feelings about everyone else in the house.

Mars was sloppy, moody and basically unserious. Lora suffered from unexplainable enthusiasms followed by total withdrawals which left her kids to fend for themselves while she disappeared into her room or out to the deck to draw. Al, although gone, was not forgotten: Nancy remembered him forever for allowing his kids to distribute randomly into every corner of the house the useless materials he brought home from scavenging trips around town. The kids were bright and charming, she admitted, but demanding and half wild at the same time. And everybody was incredibly, insupportably noisy all the time.

I started to avoid her. She was leaving and I was staying, and I didn't want to be dragged into her partisan history with her roommates. Anyway, extreme mood shifts, to take one example, seemed to me normal behavior; it was the boring in-between that had to be avoided. Tall, blonde Nancy from San Jose and her organic consort Lance from Bakersfield were never going to understand that. God bless the California Buddhists, but they're an uncomplicated lot, with their yoga and their mantras and their clear skin and unconflicted eyes. They don't know the dark and terrifying tunnels of ambiguity that New Yorkers are born understanding.

So I left it alone, feeling closer to Lora and her kids, to Mars, even to Al in his absence than I did to Lance and Nancy, even though Lance and Nancy were careful to straighten up after themselves and had a spiritual discipline, shining complexions, soft tones, narrow bones. I liked them well enough, and I was even sorry to see them go, but I knew I wasn't going to miss them.

No longer "in care of" anyone but a bonafide resident of San Francisco, I fixed up my room to represent me: a bed and a writing table, a beat-up dresser, a Barcalounger donated by a client of Moving with Mars, a sea-blue rug in which to set the discrete islands of my furniture, and floral curtains for the windows.

"The perfect neo-hippie poet's den," nodded Mars, surveying my kingdom. "Now all you need is a girlfriend."
The thought had occurred to me.

I should say that Lora was not a possibility. She had apologized nicely to me in the matter of the cashews, and now she loaned me a landscape for the wall of my room. We were friendly house companions, and I had grown to like her kids and to count them, too, as friends. I admired her lost and fertile look, but I was home free in San Francisco and the last thing I wanted was another smart, sharp, vulnerable-aggressive New York Jewish girl, let alone one who lived in the same house. If I hankered, it was for a smooth-limbed California girl, a delicatessen I had never known.
California was my true *goldineh medinah*, the golden land of dreams. I had no more begun to contemplate my desire than it was served up to me, hot and ready to eat.

Yes, the Poet's careless drifting surpasses the Ordinary Man's careful plan.
Here came Sally, a soft-mouthed junior librarian. I met her at a party and took her home across the Bay Bridge to her bachelorette in Berkeley. Since it was late, she made a bed for me against the far wall, opened her convertible couch for herself, turned out the light. We chatted in the dark about Edna St. Vincent Millay, then she joined me softly in the darkness. Ah!
For three weeks we counted the times we had made love, ending each count by adding another to the list. But after three weeks, our accounts differed and she began to complain, wanting more than I wanted to give. Without regrets, I let her swim back into the great pool of fish.
Then came Tiffany—Tiffany!—blonde and smooth-legged in tennis whites. She played a game that kept me running breathlessly back and forth on my side of the net (something about a college boy she was pledged to in Connecticut). She had two roommates who sat disapprovingly on the sidelines like cold-eyed Spanish aunts. She let pass too many serves of mine, too many easy lobs she failed to return. I slammed her finally one day, forcing the issue, but she wouldn't play with me after that, and I departed, feeling shaken by another failure of love; I hadn't thought anything like that could happen in California.
And then came my perfect slithy synthesis, the one I had

been waiting for: slow, sultry eyes, lips plump and spoiled, hair like honey pouring down the sides of her face. She was lanky in sandals, full bodied in loose cotton shifts.

I had dreamed on the Lower East Side of such a California Girl, and now here she was, a secretary at a hardware company Mars and I were moving-and-hauling across town. She showed us what to take away with efficient indifference and a private half smile to let us know that she included herself with us on the same side of some private equation. It was a genital smile.

We took two desks and a set of bookcases from the main office on Embarcadero to the branch office on Divisadero. I spent the whole drive staring out the window. *What's your name? April. What's yours? Abner. Would you like to escape this place forever? I would,* she said, *but not in a moving and hauling truck.* (Witty enough but bad for my ego.) The swing of her under her skirt, ringing with promises—

"Go get 'er, boy," said Mars.

"I wouldn't even know how to begin."

Mars looked at me like Mr. Natural regarding Shuman the Human. Then he waved his hand. "Never mind. You're right. She's unattainable. An impossible dream." He pulled at his beard. "Better look elsewhere, that's my advice."

"Oh, *psychology*, huh?" I called her that afternoon and met her for lunch the next day. While she tongued her frozen yogurt, she told me her dream was to canoe down the Russian River to the Coast, then motor northward in her little Morris Minor through the Redwood country, camping out.

A New York girl tells you about her "career;" even I, the saintly drifter, had my literary identity for a cover story. But April was a daughter of the West, free of ambition, full of dreams. The great whale of love spouted in my heart.

We became lovers. Who could believe that the Universe would be so perfectly responsive as to fast-forward me to my heart's true desire. Yes, it looked as though I would not have to make any compromise with life at all. *April, I love you. Oh, Abner, I love you too.* Poetry perfect, the ripe fruit had dropped into my hand.

I hardly went home any more. I worked with Mars, wandered downtown till it was time to meet her after work, then flew with her across the Golden Gate in that little car shaped like a derby hat, chased her up the wooden staircase to her attic room and tumbled her into bed.

We planned our getaway—a month's vacation, driving north, canoeing west, finding the place where waters meet. It was possible, probable, plausible, plentiful. My heart expanded, nearly mad with rejoicing: Poet Triumphant, Poet with long-haired, long-legged, long-fingered blonde. Behind the wheel, with an innocent boyish gesture, she hikes her skirt up for comfort, affording me a glimpse of thigh, then turns to me with a lascivious grin—and we're off.

One of her housemates was a mechanic named Eddie, who fixed her Morris for free when it broke down. I had met him once or twice *en passant* as April and I hurried through the house and up to her attic room, where our real life began—a wiry little fellow with a droopy counterculture mustache, not too impressive.

How could it be, then, that in her plan Eddie came along with us on our voyage downriver to the Coast?

Please, Sir, is this a joke?

No, it was her plan. Her dream of freedom included it. The three of us would lay our sleeping bags down together in the U.S. Wilderness Area. Was she crazy? How could her wonderful mouth be saying this?

I glowered at her. She admitted her sad scared mistake not to have told me before. She pleaded with me to understand: She wanted to be friends and lovers with me too. *Too* twisted into images inside me.

How could this be? I had heard the mermaids singing, each to each. Stuffing my crushed heart back into my chest, I hitchhiked back across the Golden Bridge.

In some sub-core of my brain I recognized that I had been snookered, had walked into a Venus man-trap. But now it was too late, I had become imprinted with her—her tanned legs, the scent of her, the kerchief she wore around her neck like Byron. Every time a Morris Minor cruised by, my heart lurched.

Gluttonous for humiliation, I made agonized phone calls to her. She was loving at first, then kind, then bored, then irritated. Then she hung up, leaving a buzz on the line. I hated her, yet separation increased my appetite for her. Under heavy furniture, Mars complained when I had trouble holding up my end. What could I do?—I was in love.

Love! Love love love! Lora rolled her eyes. Mars tried manfully to explain some other possibilities: mere lust, misplaced symbolism, the ways of Blondes to Man, some skunky tool she was using on the mechanic. Eli and Ella began making fun of me, singsonging the names of the months: "Thirty days has September, May, June, and November. We're afraid to say April because Abner gets depressed."

Defeat of my boyhood. Defeat of my dream.

And yet, once I let her, my jealous Cyna kept me company more than before, to teach me again that setbacks in the wars of romance may constitute victories in another place. Angrier now and wiser, my notebook ready in its holster, I prowled the streets of San Francisco. I sat alone at bars, taking notes for poems while nursing a beer. In short, I led the lonely writer's life. In the eternally heroic gesture of the Poet, out of misery I made songs.

Weeks went by. Coming full circle, I felt my strength return. I limped a little, yes, but I was myself again, a member of Mars's little family of friends. In the mornings, I worked with Mars, growing flat-bellied and muscular from the daily lifting and carrying. In the afternoons I wandered with my pen, and late in the day I returned home to the camaraderie of our house on the hill.

I was reading Blake then and the Romantic poets, and my belief, seasoned by Allen Ginsberg, was that a poet was meant to be a prophet and a visionary and that the doorway to the world of visions is through mundane objects and events. I forgot my personal sorrow. Telephone and refrigerator became the subjects of my poems, snatches of conversations overheard in bus and cafe, the events of our little household. I wrote poems about putting Eli and Ella to bed and about the blackberry vines that grew wild around the sheds outside the back door of the house and about the view of the towers of the Golden Gate Bridge from the top of the Bernal Heights hill.

I sent the poems out to little magazines, where they were published. Letters came back from editors, thanking me for saying what was on their minds too.

And meanwhile I continued, without realizing it, to fall in love with Lora Sachsman. And with her kids.

CHAPTER 6

One day I came back early from my private wandering and found Lora pouring milk for Eli and Ella, who were blowing into their glasses through straws while she did it, making the milk foam up and threatening to tip the glasses. "Stop it, Eli," Lora was saying. "Stop it. *Ella*!"

"Howdy," I said in my cowboy mode, coming in. "How ya doin'?"

She turned, milk container in her hand like a six-gun and regarded me tight-faced for a moment. "I am exhausted and bummed out," she said, enunciating carefully. "My husband recently abandoned me, I don't have *any* money and I spent the whole morning being treated like *shit* to get on Welfare." Eli and Ella immediately settled into taking polite little sips of milk through their straws while they looked back and forth from their mother to me.

"Ah," I said.

"You want to hear about Welfare?" She didn't wait for an answer. "First of all, it takes an hour on the fucking *bus* to get downtown. Did you ever spend an hour on a city bus with two kids? Then we get there and there's nothing to do but sit around in a big room filled with a lot of *very* creepy people." She enumerated them on her fingers. "There's the winos, the general crazies, small and very tough-looking Mexican guys, big and very tough-looking black guys, derelicts, people missing limbs, a squad of guys who blow their noses into their hands, a few string-haired hippie types in training to be full-fledged derelicts and bag ladies, plus a lot of very stupid-looking overweight women of all races with five kids under the age of two climbing all over each of them."

"And there was a guy who peed in his pants," said Eli rhapsodically.

"We saw him do it," added Ella.

"You sure did," agreed Lora. "And the room is very warm—so smells rise, okay? And Eli and Ella are slightly terrified and totally bored, because there's nothing to do. Then, after an hour and a half, we get called by our social worker, who turns out to be a middle-aged black woman who doesn't like us and gets mad at Eli for asking questions about everything on her desk—"

"There was a rock that looked like a cat," Ella volunteered.
"It was a sculpture," explained Eli, "and it was—"
"—And who gets angry at me to me because I haven't filled out one of the forms. And then, when it's all done, for a *really special treat*, we get to go home on the bus again. So how do you think I'm doing? And what the hell are you grinning about?"

I was enjoying the show. I recognized Lora—an earnest, brash, neurotic New York girl. I grinned at the kids and the kids grinned back.

Lora heaved a sigh, as if she had gotten something off her chest. "Well," she said self-mockingly, "*now* I feel better." And for that moment, when we looked around, there we were, all smiling at one another.

Ella was just under five years old then, dark-eyed and plump, with a full, pouty mouth and a hint of precocious sexuality in her baby fat. Strong-willed and capable of stubborn refusals, she was also a wise-hearted listener, one of those children you can have a conversation with. She knew how to play quietly while the grownups talked about grownup things and possessed a savvy sense of when a question might be appropriate and when it would get her remembered and banished.

Eli, on the other hand, was—a seven-year-old *boy*. He played noisy car games or made a mess trying to see what color he would get if he mashed all his crayons together or wanted to know how sand gets made into glass, in detail. His ideas about personal grooming were primitive, and for long periods of time he refused to let Lora cut his hair, which kept flopping down in front of his eyes. He also developed the awful habit of chewing on his shirt cuffs, which left them hanging off his wrists in wet shreds. He looked like a raggamuffin street urchin, but there was something solid and manly about him, and he was very smart.

As soon as I had become a provisional member of the household, apparently trusted by Lora and Mars, the children inducted me into their going-to-bed ritual, asking me to take my turn with a story, a song, the recapitulation of the day's events or anything else that would extend bedtime a few extra minutes. I became proficient in those early days at reading while rotating the book like radar so the children, trusting and fragrant in their beds, could receive the pictures.

The kids soon made assumptions about the availability of my lap as a place to sit, trusted me to soothe a hurt or keep a secret, invited me to the funeral of a butterfly that had fallen to earth. I counted them among my friends.

I would oblige Ella with one of her favorite activities, called "walk-and-talk," in which we would go around the block (or sometimes just around the house) discussing anything we thought of. Eli and I founded a household newspaper, *The Weekly Halliday*, named for our street, which included such headlined features as, "Mars breaks Ella's favorite bowl," "Lora gets diarrhea from Abner's tomato soup," and "Mars stays at Rabbit's three nights in a row."

At the kitchen table, Lora and I exchanged life stories.

She had been born in the Bronx, but her family had moved to the New Jersey suburbs when she was still at a tender age. "I was a child artist in the suburbs," she told me. "I almost got thrown out of school at the age of ten for drawing a picture of a girl with breasts. They called my mother to come and talk to the teacher. You weren't allowed to have breasts in those days—that was before sex was so prevalent."

At seventeen, a freshman at Cooper Union, Lora met Al, a sophomore. Love, need and recklessness combined—at nineteen, she became pregnant. "Al wouldn't consider an abortion—'life-defying' was the expression he used. He kept telling me not to worry, that everything would work out great. So we got married. We wanted to elope, but my mother wanted the whole shmear—a big wedding, me in a white gown. She even came over to counsel me about first-night sex."

"She didn't know you were sleeping together?"

Lora rolled her eyes. "We had *lived* together the year before. Al and I had gone to Europe together one summer. When I was sixteen, my mother found my diaphragm in my drawer. But now she decided I was a virgin again. That was the time I finally confronted the fact that my mother is out of touch. I'm telling her I think I might want to call the wedding off—call off the caterer and the rabbi and *everything*—and she's hugging me and crooning in my ear, 'Oh *darling*, I'm so *happy* for you.' Really."

"Wow," I obliged softly.

Lora nodded and shrugged. "You see, all my life she had wanted me to be a particular kind of daughter, a particular kind of *person*—someone she could show off to her friends and go shopping with—and I wasn't it. I was the wrong person. But this time she was going make me *be* it, even if she had to disconnect from reality. And take me to lala land with her." She paused, and I could feel the anger and the sarcasm melt partly into sadness. "I never really got taken care of, you know," she said.

"You want a cup of tea?" I asked solicitously.

That made her laugh. "Sure," she said, and I rose to put the kettle on.

After the wedding, Lora dropped out of Cooper Union. Eli was born six months later. "My mother told her friends and relatives he was premature. For months after he was born, she wouldn't let me visit her because she was afraid the neighbors would figure it out."

I poured hot water into our cups. Lora seemed suddenly to be staring at something next to her on the table. Then, as if there was nothing strange or sublime about the transition, she got up abruptly, took her big purse off the counter, withdrew pen and notebook from it, sat down again and began to draw the reflection of her cup in the little puddle of water I had spilled on the table while pouring the tea. The distorted surfaces of the teacup developed rapidly in black and white on the white sheet.

"Where was I?" she asked finally.

"Having a baby."

"Oh, right. Then I got pregnant again. It was unplanned, but I wouldn't exactly call it a *surprise*. I mean, if your protest against feeling trapped in your life takes the form of ignoring birth control, how surprised can you *be* when you get pregnant?"

After Ella's birth, Al set up his own business as a photographer, which had long been an interest of his. They accepted some financial help from her parents, but it had a price. While Al was out trying to sell himself for weddings and bar mitzvahs, her parents paid unannounced visits. They had moved to the suburbs to escape city scenes much more benign than the ones outside Lora's windows, and they were horrified by how Lora and Al lived.

"'Filthy-dirty,'" Lora said in a witch voice, poking a bony finger at me. "'Everything was 'filthy-dirty.' I mean, maybe she had a point about me letting Eli shit on the floor—"

"You let him shit on the floor?"

"I let him go naked because it was easier to clean the floors than to wash diapers. But she even got hysterical once because Ella was wearing unmatched socks. 'How could you *do* this to me? What did I do to deserve this?' And my father, who I thought I could count on to be *rational*—he agreed with her, as if I was inflicting some sort of permanent psychological damage on Ella by letting her wear one yellow sock and one black one.

"But the *weirdest* part," Lora went on, "was that my parents wouldn't ever sit down in my apartment because everything was so 'filthy-dirty,' so their visits with all this yelling and screaming happened *standing up*."

While she talked, she had made two quick sketches of the bowl of walnuts that occupied the center of the table. Now she settled into a full portrait while she described how she and Al, with two little kids and no money, began to dream in the bohemian slums of New York about the country. "It was mostly Al's dream at first," she explained. "He was into the practical farm-and-animal aspect of it."

"But not you."

"I was into the being-in-the-country-with-other-people-and-having-time-to-paint aspect of it." The nuts as she drew them were more creviced, fleshy and complex than the nuts on the table—sexual nuts. "Al would come home from the library, push his desk in front of the air-shaft window and learn composting and goat birthing out of books. Friends in Oregon were writing to us about clean air and group child care. One day we just decided to *go*—packed everything in boxes, tied it on top of our old Volvo and went. We called it dropping out the bottom of dropping out."

"You lived on a hippie commune?" I was impressed.

"Oh, yeah. And I loved it at first," Lora said. "Gardening and living in a place where, when you walked out of your door you were outside—no five flights of smelly stairs. I didn't have to worry about my kids every second, and there were other people to help take care of them. My mother had been *telling* me to get out of the slums, so—" She turned up a hand.

"You're a dutiful daughter."

"Always."

But residence in Paradise was followed by problems in Paradise, then bummers in Paradise, then Fall and Exile. There was no hot water and no telephone and no money. In the winter, it rained all the time and the cabins were so cold that you could see your breath when you got in bed. "Al was *building* the greenhouse and *fixing* cars and *planting* the garden and *digging* the well—it got so I couldn't have a conversation with him any more, his vocabulary had *dwindled* so much. I mean, you get tired of talking about chickenshit and organic broccoli, right?"

"I'm tired of it already," I assured her.

"Al and I weren't getting along too well. We decided to have an 'open marriage' and be friends and adults and not be possessive any more. It was all supposed to be good for us. We put our sleeping bags on opposite sides of the meadow. Al had an affair with a woman named Sharon Bird who had a pet rat that lived in her hair." She looked me in the eye. "I'm *not* kidding," she said. "And I had one with Sharon Bird's ex-old man. He was a mechanic and smelled of gasoline all the time. I was afraid if I lit a match I would kill him."

She shook her head, then turned the page and began doing quick sketches of me, looking in quick succession up at me and down at the page. "Not being possessive—the strain of that was a *killer*—it's just not my nature. And we couldn't really break up because we had two kids to take care of. *Then* people began to complain I was spending too much of my time making art." She frowned at her drawing and turned the page again. "And Al said he *sort of* understood what they meant. I couldn't *believe* it! Al and I had always agreed that my work would be a priority for both of us." She looked speculatively at me, pen poised for a moment, then dived in again.

"Meanwhile, Al had put his whole heart and soul into communal projects—he'd planted *half* the fucking garden by himself and done most of the work on a new irrigation system and gotten elbow deep in breech-birth goats—he did *everything*. But when he wanted to try out his ideas for French composting and geodesic domes, the other guys said no, it was a waste of time or materials or money or energy." She paused to take a breath. "So you might say that by our second summer, we were drifting out of *kinship* with our communal brothers and sisters. It was time to leave, but we couldn't agree where to go. Is this even slightly interesting to you?"

Is was not so much the story as the sweep and lilt of her New York diction that were interesting to me, as well as the gossamers of hair along the slope of her neck, the movement of the tendons in her hand as she drew. “Yes, I’m very interested,” I told her.

“Well, you’re not responding a lot.” Drawing, she didn’t look up. “I need you to ‘Uh huh’ every once in a while—I’m very insecure.”

“Uh huh.”

“Good. Al’s idea was to move up to an abandoned mining claim in the mountains. It was so remote, the road to get there was only wide enough for half a car, and then you climbed down a slope to a cabin that had no running water and no electricity, not even an outhouse. Oh, it had an extravagant and emerald wild beauty,” she said as if quoting Irish poetry. “Of course I *absolutely* refused to live there.”

His second plan was the ashram in British Columbia—“far from everything in the world with a lot of Hindus or Buddhists running around in salmon togas and shaved heads, chanting mantras and eating seaweed.” She rolled her eyes like Eddie Cantor—like Ella, I mentioned to myself.

So they had come to San Francisco, back to the city; she had won. But by then they were exhausted from disagreeing. “Our marriage kept unraveling but it didn’t quite dissolve, and in a way we got along fine—Al and I always got along fine. We just didn’t talk to each other any more.” She looked down at the drawing again, up at me, up and down and up, making quick finished strokes, an edge of her lips pinned by her teeth, concentrating. She tilted her head to look, then turned it around for me to see.

It was someone with a high forehead and the beginnings of a beard, but not me. “It doesn’t look much like me,” I had to say.

“It’ll take me a while to get you,” she agreed. “You have a good face,” she said, turned another page and began to draw again.

The conversation went on for weeks, like a floating craps game. In the morning I worked, in the afternoon I wandered, but I came home a little earlier each day. Alone in my room, I discovered words shaped like pictures swimming in currents under the surface of my desk. And even when, as happened some days, the energy disappeared and the world’s events and objects dropped into randomness, without metaphor or meaning, leaving me limp and despairing, I could relearn to nurse the gift back or wrestle it flat onto a sheet of paper and emerge the conquerer.

Lora understood this. We would sit at the kitchen table over cups of tea or go out on the sun deck behind the house and talk. Fellow artist, she opened her notebooks for me, and I paged through them, amazed to find my own face and hand recorded there, along with the likenesses of Mars, Nancy, Lance, Al, Ella and Eli, others I did not know, as well as clarified images from our household life.

One day we sat, surrounded by wild blackberry vines, on the sun deck next to the sheds behind the house, and Lora opened for me her older sketchbooks. I found in them images I thought I had invented in dreams: reflections of landscapes in the wing-mirror of a car; one detail on a cluttered table became the center point of a dinner party; a yellow Volvo piled high with belongings, foreshortened as it headed down a windy road into the woods.

She turned the pages for me one by one: little oil-crayon drawings and collages, delicate fingertips of color, drawn shapes balanced mysteriously on each other, black and white renderings of ordinary objects, my own face, my hand at rest. I watched her fingers as she turned the pages and it was like walking through her mind and finding myself there.

"It's like another world in your drawings," I told her, impressed.

"It's definitely not my real world," she said regretfully.

"I think it is your real world," I told her. "It's the rest of the world that's not real."

"I like your point of view," said Lora.

So that's how it went: After work and wandering in the afternoon, I came home and hung out with Lora and her kids in the afternoon. I told her the story of my life too: Born in Brooklyn, a grocer's son; overprotected by my mother, neglected by my father, bullied by my older brother. Dreamy, full of tears and longing, I had marched through the Public School and the Synagogue School, learning to be bored, to be baffled, to stand in line, to pass for normal while lost in wondering how to connect what I felt in my heart to how the world was formed and what shape it was that girls carried between their thighs.

"Did you learn about the shape?" Lora asked.

"Ah, the shape," I sighed. Lora had a focused interest in the women I had dated, and I obliged it, from nice Lillian, the high school pal who had allowed my hand under her brassiere one night on Ocean Parkway all the way to Amy Solomon, from whom I had fled New York.

"Amy Solomon?" Lora sprang to alertness. Her eyes got distant as she went through a file in her mind. She found something. "A busty girl with a wide smile? Her father sells lingerie?" She pronounced it *longzhuray*.

"Her uncle. You know her?"

"I met her once. Al had a friend who knew her sister. I once got two brassieres at a discount through her. So what happened with you and Amy Solomon?"

Amy Solomon was a brainy as well as busty girl, with a round face and an agile body. I had loved her from the days when I first sat behind her in Art History, eyeing the profile of her breasts. We had become friends slowly, then dear friends, then, unable to stand mere friendship any more, I had insisted with her against a schoolyard fence in Brooklyn until she accepted my lips on hers. Sweetheart, and friends, we went on afternoon walks and evening dates, spent weekends in one another's company and at last lived together in a railroad flat on Second Street. So many wonderful things had happened between us, miracles of intimate communication and a lot of good sex.

And then we broke up. Telling Lora about it, I could not quite say why we had half begun to hate each other, why disagreements about whether to open or close the window flowered into huge raw fights. It got worse and worse, but even then we couldn't let go of each other simply. We ended living in separate apartments but still dating.

It was horrible. Now I came to *visit* her. When the phone rang, she would speak a few moments in the other room, and when she came back she wouldn't say who it had been. One night while she was in the bathroom—I found myself confessing the worst to Lora—I had gone looking for her diaphragm, wanting to *know*. It was not in the top drawer of her dresser, where she always kept it, nor in the drawers I hurried my hands through. I had found it at last in her purse, at rest in its plastic case, powdered dully with corn starch, blandly uncommunicative. O nauseous rage! "How bad love smells when it goes bad!" I cried to Lora at the kitchen table. "And after that I began to run into her on Eighth Street with her arms around a stranger." I shook my head. "Some people never learn their lesson," I sighed dramatically.

"You still love Amy Solomon?"

"No," I said. Love her? I had dismissed her forever from my life. And yet the question sent a sharp spear of regret and longing through me. Did I, underneath it all, still long for Amy Solomon? She had once made me happy, had once been my darling friend. Maybe I still loved that Amy—Amy *then.* "Maybe in a way," I confessed. "But it's a way that's more about unhappiness than about having fun together."

"Al and I didn't even have fights any more," she volunteered. "We were just together—we even had fun together sometimes. But we didn't really care any more, we were just very *involved* with each other."

She fell silent, and then two tears crept out of her eyes, and she began to cry in slow motion, not hiding it, making wet half-sounds, her eyes on her fingers in her lap. My heart expanded, hot with sympathy, but I did not know what to do except to sit beside her while she wept. When she was finished, she wiped her hand across her face and sniffled, then turned to me again, her face softened, and gave a little embarrassed laugh. "Thank you," she said.

"You're welcome," I answered, meaning it.

Thus, very politely and more each day, we became friends. Recovering from my defeat in the Romance Wars, I limped home each afternoon from Wandering, seeking the comfort of our conversations, with their combination of silliness and depth and their easy intimacy, as well as the warm domesticity of doing projects with the kids, reading to them, exploring with them, putting them to bed the way they taught me to—being a family.

I began to depend on them all being there when I got home.

CHAPTER 7

Lora kept the kids out of school so the System couldn't make soldiers out of them. In the afternoons, I would write for a while, then, while Lora painted, I would pack a snack and go for a walk-and-talk with them. Usually we trekked no further than the top of the steps at the end of Halliday Avenue. There was freeway construction going on below us. Basking in that special sense of wisdom one gets from elevation, we ate our apple slices and invented stories about the workers in their orange vests.

To the sausage-shaped foreman, we gave a skinny wife who loved her husband so much that she only cooked food that reminded her of him—frankfurters, thick salamis, knockwurst, bananas for dessert. We called them the Tube family. To the bearded longhair we ascribed the custom of giving away joints to the other workers, a habit that annoyed the aristocratic Mexican, who had a slight crookedness in his walk—remnant of an injury suffered during his days as a bullfighter. We laughed a lot.

By the time the workmen slouched back to their trucks to put their tools away, Lora would have joined us with her sketchbook to record the men closing up the site, the aerial cityscape that stretched all the way to the Bay, the loops of the highway, the yellow bulldozers and the orange hauling trucks and tractors. Her idea, she said, marveling at the urban beauty, was a series of paintings called "Men at Work."

So we sat for a half hour or more, talking about whatever came into our heads and paying easy attention to ourselves or each other. Those were healing and nutritive times.

Eli had roller skates, the kind that were built as part of the shoes. He offered to teach Ella to skate, but she claimed his method was to stand in front of her and say, "Come on now, skate!" She would fall immediately and after a while wouldn't try any more, partly because she didn't like putting on his shoes—not only were they too big on her, but they had his cooties. But when he went out on the street to skate, she complained.

I took it on myself to be her trainer, first convincing her that an extra pair of socks would make the shoes fit better and keep her free of cooties. Then we went out in front of the house. First I had her stand still in her skates, allowing her to grab onto me when she felt herself sliding. Then we walked together a while, me holding her hand while she slip-slid beside me, giving small cries of alarm. That was the first day.

The second day, the real lessons began. I had to insist that Eli go into the house. He had come out to sit on the steps and kept offering advice. This infuriated Ella, even though it was generally pretty good advice about not watching her feet and pointing one toetip to the ground to stop her slide.

After Eli went in the house, she stood in the skates (taking Eli's advice about toe placement). I stood a couple of steps in front of her and challenged her to get to my outstretched hands without falling.

"It's an important lesson you're about to learn, Ella," I assured her. "You're going to jump over the abyss of your fear." She looked at me with big brown eyes, and I believe she understood. "Come on," I said, feeling a little like I was being God, training her for the leap of faith, to expand, despite fear, into her own real capabilities. Come on, little sister, the water's fine.

She fell, landing heavily on her palms and one knee. I scooped her back onto her feet in an instant, not giving her time to decide if tears were necessary, brushed her off and told her, "Try again." This time she made it; skated clumsily the length of two short strides and fell into my arms. Then she did it again, her face beginning to glow with accomplishment.

Day by day, we extended the distance she dared to skate. Soon she had enough skill to do it on her own: She had learned to skate.

And I had learned to take the time to get down on my knees to be a compatible height and to bestow a hug of comfort or congratulations, as I had learned over the weeks to cure child crankiness by a moment's direct energy. Most important of all, I had allowed myself to be drawn into the world of play.

What better training can a poet have?

After he left, Al Rosen didn't keep in great contact with his wife and children. The first time I met him, I had been a visitor, a new arrival in his home. The next time, I had a room of my own and was busy making friends with his family. Maybe he felt odd about that. Maybe that was why he blew in and stayed only one day, sleeping on the living room couch, as I had at the beginning.

He borrowed Mars's van and took a trip around town, returning with, among other things, two cartons of styrofoam packing material, which Eli and Ella manically scattered into all the corners of every room. As a show of good will, Al spent most of the evening of his visit picking them up by hand, one at a time, like an amphetamine addict lifting lint out of a carpet.

At the ashram, he had risen to be aide to the lady swami. He was proud of himself and full of stories about her miraculous ability, which he had witnessed at first hand, to relieve the physical suffering of others by accepting it on herself. "It weakens her but she wants to do it," he explained over dinner.

"Does she have children to support?" asked Lora.

The next morning he left on foot, after hugging and waving bye-bye to his children. His plan was to hitchhike back to Canada. Mars, who happened to be standing on the front steps drinking his second cup of coffee, saw him pass by the house again a half hour later, going the other way. He had decided to hitchhike to Los Angeles for a while instead, he said, and was gone.

And Ella cried bitterly in bed all day. When Mars and I got home from work she was still there, the pillow damp around her face, sobbing for her daddy.

"Did you ask him if he was planning to stop off here again on his way back from L.A.?" Lora asked, distraught. Mars hadn't, and Al hadn't volunteered the information.

Ella kept expecting Al each day for two weeks, wanting her daddy back, but he didn't come.

The next time we heard from him, it was raining in San Francisco. Long days of heavy mist were followed by nights of downpour. Al called from Oregon and said he would be down for Ella's birthday with a special present for her. Ella's birthday came—she spent most of it with her nose pressed against the front window, looking out into the grayness—and went. He didn't appear. In the evening, still expecting him at any moment, we had her party, with chocolate cake by Lora and gifts from all of us. Mars pulled on an old clown suit and clowned. Rabbit did magic tricks. It was nice but hollow, and Ella stayed withdrawn and moody, going through with it as if only to please us. It was pouring outside, and she was five years old.

He didn't come the next day, or the next, and he didn't call. A week later, he showed up, lugging along with him a truly beautiful oak jewelry case that he had made by hand for her. She was thrilled with it and leapt up into his arms: "Daddy, Daddy, Daddy." She made sure he got something to eat, then proudly trotted out for dessert the piece of her birthday cake which she had saved for him in the refrigerator. It was dried out and sad-looking, but he thanked her, tears in his eyes, and ate it all while everybody watched. And then, both his children dancing around his knees, Al took them into their room to entertain and cuddle and put them to bed.

I had never before seen this narrow, grim look on Lora's face. "That bastard," she said.

He stayed three days this time, sleeping on the living room couch or between Eli's and Ella's beds, like the third kid in the house. And then he was gone again and the kids were crazy.

"That bastard," Lora said for the twentieth time. "He comes late, he breaks her heart, he brings *her* a gift but nothing for Eli, and then he leaves and *I* have to pick up the pieces." Ella brought the jewelry box out of her room to show it off for the hundredth time. "It's really beautiful, sweetheart," Lora told her. "Yes, your daddy made it himself, just for you."

Eli was standing in the doorway, idly chewing on the cuff of his long-sleeved polo shirt. "I want to go out for a hamburger," he said suddenly to his mother.

"Not now, Eli," I heard Lora tell him as I made my way back to my room, where I was educating a poem toward maturity. He said again, louder, "I want to go out for a hamburger."

The rest of what happened came to me through the walls of my room. Lora must have said no, because he began yelling and screaming at the top of his lungs that he wanted to go out for a hamburger. When I say yelling and screaming, I am not using a stock phrase. Yelling has words; screaming has only sounds. Eli did them both, over and over, until, through the wall, I began to hear an overlay of Lora's voice as well, telling him to shut up.

Then there was a brief silence, and then Lora was shouting, "I can't take it any more! When do *I* get taken care of? *When do I get taken care of?*" Sounds of chairs scraping, fists banging on a table, feet running down the foyer; sobbing; quiet.

I sat at my desk, reliving traumatic scenes from my own childhood, with their deep resonances of guilt and remorse. I already had one lesson from Lora about staying out of her family dramas, but that was before we had become friends.

I felt a calling.

When I opened my door, Eli scared me by being right there in the hallway like an eavesdropper. He had a tragic look on his little boy's face; the chewed wet end of sleeve hung off his wrist like an amputation. "You want to come in?" I invited. He shrugged as if he didn't care, but came.

He looked at a lot of things—books on the shelf, the coins and keys beside my bed, the road map of the U.S.A. on the wall—but not at me.

"You feeling bad?" I suggested, sitting down behind my desk.

"I hate her," he informed me.

We are so helpless when we are little. "It's a hard time for your Mom too," I tried. "She loves you and wants to take care of you."

"Then why does she *hit*?" he demanded hotly, turning away so I wouldn't see him cry.

"Oh, Eli," I said, into the moist atmosphere of the room. Lora was ideologically opposed to spanking; she must be *in extremis*. Remembering the heavy slap and the helpless hurting from my own boyhood, my heart filled with a pain that was not only Eli's. I found myself nodding, my whole body empathetic.

Thus, when I spoke, my words, though common, felt to me inspired as well, because I could be parent and child at the same time—two things at once, as poets love to be. "Oh, Eli," I repeated, "people try their best but sometimes they blow it. You know that." I waited but he didn't say anything. "People blow it," I said again. "I do, you do, Lora does, Ella does—Al does."

"I hate her," he said again.

He looked so manly and so ridiculous, a little guy standing there with his wet sleeves hanging down, his long hair half over his eyes, serious as a refugee. He let me squat down next to him and put my hand on his shoulder. "Let's go talk to your Mom about it, okay?"

His face darkened and he shook his head no.

"I'll go with you," I offered. "We'll work it out and make it be okay," I assured him, bullying him through his disbelief. "I'll go with you."

I offered him my hand. He gave a bare nod. He took my hand and we went to talk to Lora.

In the kitchen, Lora's face was swimming around on the front of her head and changing colors—she was as upset as her skin was capable of articulating.

"What's going on?" I asked.

"Nothing," she said. "I've just had it, that's all."

"IT ISN'T MY FAULT!" Eli suddenly yelled beside me.

His shout left a kind of hole in the air through which Lora and I both looked at him, surprised, then back at each other. Eli stormed out of the room, too overcome with his confession to face us, and we heard the door slam to the kids' room.

Lora rubbed her cheeks. "He thinks it's his fault. I think it's my fault. I guess Ella thinks it's her fault." She paused, sighed. "I've got to go talk with them."

"You want me to come along?"

"Would you? You're a sane influence on us all."

I squatted down against one wall of the kids' room while Lora apologized for flying off the handle, for yelling, for smacking Eli, reassuring them it wasn't their fault. Ella, lying in her bed, remained inaccessible, her face to the wall, mourning. Eli was tearing with his teeth the huge red apple he had grabbed on his way out of the kitchen, grunting as he chewed and swallowed. The rain had stopped, and the twilight air beyond the windows was quiet and misty. Except for Ella's and Eli's separate small-animal noises, everything was silent. "Oh boy," Lora said with a note of panic in her voice, "another evening."

Something in me recognized that the solution might be up to me. Perhaps I had been brought here just for that reason. Poet is priest. So in the darkening room I made a little impromptu and platitudinous sermon about how when people cared about each other, having hard times just gave them the chance to be stronger and more loving.

Because I sounded certain, they believed me. Lora promised Eli never to hit any more; they hugged and forgave. Only Ella wouldn't relent. Lora sat beside her and stroked her hair and whispered to her, but her heart was broken and she didn't care. She wouldn't even look at me.

Too much had happened for me to go back to my desk. I was filled up with the possibilities for caring, for giving and for mattering that these people's lives offered me. Not words on paper here, but the real flesh of the world.

"Are you kids hungry?" Lora asked.

"I want noodles," Eli said.

"Go away," said Ella.

With faith in carbohydrates to repair hurts, Lora and I made a meal. Ella refused to join us. Mars was at Rabbit's—they had been having couple trouble for weeks and he was (I thought) insisting on being with her more than was strategic. He said he had to try. We left a plate of food beside Ella's bed and ate alone, just the three of us. Afterward Lora and I did the dishes together.

I am sitting in front of my typewriter, retyping a poem. Ella comes in and leans against my shoulder. After a moment, she says, "I know how to make poems on a typewriter."

"How?" I ask her.

"Don't look at what keys you're pressing," says the little Zen master, "*and type fast.*"

That was the other side of Ella. She sat with me and Lora beside the house while we talked about death. Suddenly she said, "I just died for a minute."

"What was it like?" Lora asked her.

"The grass was me," she explained solemnly. She giggled. We both stared at her in awe—the five-year-old perfect master.

That winter, Mars broke up with Rabbit. His heart, searching for the perfect vaudevillean two-step, found the disappointment hard to understand. "I thought I was done looking for a while," he told me, tears welling up. We spent whole nights talking it through, with me saying back to him many of the same things he had said to me when my heart split on the sharp reef of April. He understood it all.

But understanding is a tool, not a remedy. With Rabbit gone, Mars developed an urge for travel again. "If I stay in San Francisco, I'll get cynical," he said.

He took it slow, researching a destination, giving me time to find another job, waiting for us to find a replacement for him in the house. I found a job as a schoolyard recreation director, playing basketball with twelve-year-olds and supervising playground and equipment in the afternoons after school. I had to change my schedule around, but I still had half the day for writing and wandering, I could still pursue as my quirky career the creation of the life I liked to live, which was (as Lora and I agreed), a basic job of Artist in Society.

Reading Blake and the Romantics, along with Ginsberg and Aldous Huxley's books about religion and visionary experience, what I preached from my bully pulpit was my own Jewish/Blakean vision of the world riddled with ecstasy and the poet's role as prophet and visionary. It seemed so obvious to me that the door to the other world opened through mundane objects, events and relationships.

In those months, I wrote poems about caring for the children and the small events of our household; about sitting in sunshine among the blackberry vines behind the house; about the pest-control man, who came to eradicate a plague of silverfish and departed through the middle of the nasturtium bed that Mars and Rabbit had planted—the compleat Exterminator. In short, I continued to try to convert into poesy the small events of my day.

I liked my thoughts. I had no woman but I was not lonely. I had no money, but I felt strong and self-sufficient. Burdened with a personality, I whirred and worried too, of course, but there in that house beside the endless river of the freeway, I felt happy, someone living among his own.

Lora seemed adjusted to her new life, too. "This keeps me sane," she told me, standing in her studio room, brush in hand, face and clothing smudged with earth colors, working up one of the sketches of the freeway construction into a painting. "When I don't do it, I go crazy—that's how I know I have to do it. And when I *am* doing it, everything I'm doing every minute *is* it, because I can use everything that happens to me for making art."

"What about taking care of your kids?" I wondered.

"I can cook dinner as an artist," she said. "I can clean my kids' butts as an artist. I can take a bus ride as an artist—as long as I have the time and space to be an artist, I can accomplish everything else I need to do. Being an artist doesn't mean not functioning. It just means—well, being an artist instead of being ordinary. Right?"

Yes, right. The world is a funnel through which angels send to us, as we need it, exactly what we need to mold poems and paintings and our own precious lives. I had the dreamy gift of living on two levels, and I dwelt with Lora as if she were my sister.

We needed a new roommate. Lora found Judy, a teacher at the alternative school that, compelled by law and by her need for daytime hours to paint, Lora had decided would not harm her children. A languorous Jewish girl from Ohio, Judy had just broken up with her husband: He was getting custody of their apartment. She would be able to ferry the kids back and forth to school most of the time, she and Lora liked each other and she was fine with me.

Mars, choosing Los Angeles as his destination, had fixed up the back of his van as a living space. *Moving with Mars*, it still said on the side of the truck. The day came and I helped him load his final stuff. He hugged Lora and the kids, then he and I embraced. Now I had a beard for him to tug, too. And then he climbed behind the wheel and drove off, my Red Eminence gone out of my life for a while, though our old vow remained: that we would begin again next time where we had ended this, brothers and friends.

So the House of Mars, to which I had fled from New York almost a year before, became my home but not his.

There was an extra emptiness in the house that weekend, as Lora and I together cleaned up the emotional and material debris of Mars's leaving. I helped move the kids' beds and dresser from their room to Mars's, which was bigger, and got the kids' room ready to receive Judy, who was moving in after school on Monday.

Thus it happened, as the chain of coincidence set itself into unalterable law—by hitchhiking, so to speak—that Lora and I found ourselves for one night living alone together in that ramshackly house on a hill. The next day, when Judy moved in, we would be a commune again.

Wired with the insistent energies of Mars's leavetaking, Eli and Ella required long bedtimes from both their mother and me before they allowed Lora to shut their light. After that, unsettled and exhausted, Lora and I moped separately around the house, unable to concentrate on anything. "We need a TV," Lora suggested, and then her eyes got wide and bright, as she remembered that there now *was* a television in the corner of the living room where Judy had made a small mountain of boxes of her books and clothing. We dug it out of the pile, set it on the table in front of the living room windows and settled down.

Good old television!—small figures hurrying around telling

jokes and shooting each other for our entertainment. Sitting on the sofa, snacking and laughing and making rude comments, we switched among variety shows, sitcoms and cop shows, more and more comfortably drugged on good old teevee.

Though we had been together a lot these past few months, had laughed together, talked together, taken walks and made meals together, confided in and done favors for each other and knew each other with the intimacies one learns from living with, we had, of course, not touched.

Of course, one touches one's friends to pass them the salt, to welcome them home, to get past them in a crowded kitchen. But we had not *touched.* Many times in those weeks, I had known in a silence or a look that I might risk grazing my fingers against hers where they rested on the table. But I knew how large a change so small a gesture would bring, and refrained.

She was a slender woman with a narrow face, her eyes a changing shade of brown, with dark hair she wore either tumbled down onto her shoulders or braided in a pigtail behind her. I sat beside her in the silver light of show biz, her roommate and friend, and I had to wonder if in my careful protection of myself from the deceits of love, I had not tricked myself again. Had I been working all along to seduce Lora Sachsman and myself at the same time? Around us the house was dark and empty. Restraint had by itself become arousal.

During a commercial, Lora changed into her familiar flannel nightgown and her bathrobe. Now she sat, dressed like Mother Goose, with her legs tucked under her, brushing her hair out into a shiny semicircle on her shoulders.

Should I risk it? Would I tomorrow have to find another place to live? "Lora?" I said, my voice half a croak.

She turned to look, held my eyes a long, flat moment. I let my fingers rest on her terryclothed shin.

She put her hand over mine.

We made love slowly, as good friends should, aiming at something deeper than ecstasy-and-release, hanging out in great pleasure, laughing and talking as we went. Afterward, we lay together a long time, joined but not moving. "I love you, you know," Lora told me matter-of-factly, pulling me in further with her legs.

I hadn't known. "Don't say that," I protested, refusing the commitment.

She squeezed inside so I could feel it, a genital shrug. "I wanted you to know," she said.

O Cyna, Companion of Hitchhikers, what if the sudden turn of road should lead one home?

And while we made love, the children slept in the back bedroom of the house, not knowing that their lives were changed forever.

CHAPTER 8

From the beginning, Al did not act angry, possessive, betrayed or any of the hundred other hostile ways I would have had I come back to find my wife was lovers with someone else in what used to be my home.

"That's his religious discipline," Lora explained wearily. "He's into detachment."

Still, his routine of calling, telling us to expect him and then not showing up till days after might have been his method of revenge.

The kids would be frazzled and manic, Lora furious and distant, me perplexed. It felt as if we were all coming down with something.

And then he would show up, the children's father, of whom little was demanded and nothing expected, the flu in our family system. With him as our guest, we all got sick; all of a sudden we didn't know any more exactly who we were to one another—me least of all. Who were these people? Somebody else's wife, somebody else's kids and Somebody Else.

Nobody even questioned his right to a sleeping place in our living room. He was one of the family—we just didn't know which one. His presence gave us a built-in baby-sitter and temporary rest from child care, but there was a price: him. He raced around town in his car, bringing back discarded butt-ends of rolls of printing paper that Lora could use for large drawings, crates of half-good peaches from behind supermarkets, which he then cooked into a dozen peach pies with crusts he made from scratch, a load of used car tires which he dumped in a pile in the hilly lot outside the kitchen window but never got around to making into the playground he had projected.

On one visit, apparently sensitive to our distress at his mere presence, he collected a load of small tree branches, bent and bound them together to build a little wickiup on the empty lot beside the house, next to the mound of car tires. He covered the wickiup with elephant-fern leaves and called it home for the five days of his visit. He had a tiny cookstove out there, a radio, a wooden crate for a night table beside his sleeping bag, a big flashlight so he could read at night. The kids spent a lot of time visiting him there—"going to Al's," as it became known around the house. He explained that he didn't want to impose on our household, and no one had the heart, or the nerve, or the stomach, or the balls, or the brain to tell him that playing prophet-in-exile outside our kitchen window was itself imposition.

After Al left, the wickiup stayed, a relic of his presence in our lives. After all, were we barbarians to destroy a usable structure? The kids played in it only rarely. Weeds grew up around and over it, and it became part of the landscape, the normal view out the kitchen window while washing dishes. We accepted it as a crazy emblem of our idiosyncratic family.

In the spring, as the school year ended, our housemate Judy fell in love and made plans to follow her beloved, Lon, to Spokane. She wept to be leaving us and to be making her breakup with her husband final, but Lon made her happy: she wanted to be with him. "I'm not worried when I'm with him," she explained.

Before they departed, Lon, a tall ex-hippie who had apprenticed himself to an Indian medicine man in Spokane, blessed the corners of our house with incense smoke and eagle feathers, Eli and Ella following behind him into every room, eyes wide.

That night, Lora beamed around at us as she set the noodle casserole on the table. "Well," she said, with the sarcasm in which I knew she dressed her deepest truths, "here we are, the typical American family—Mom, Dad, Buddy and Sis."

"Except," returned Eli, "that you and Abner aren't married and Abner's not our father."

"Just what I said," his mother told him, "a typical American family."

We didn't replace Judy. We would be Mom, Dad, Buddy and Sis.

Al arrived for his next visit feeling poorly and lay on the living room couch most of the first afternoon. He accepted the kind ministrations of his children with a brave hypochondria that was the flip side of his manic enthusiasm. It was the day before Lora's twenty-sixth birthday, and after dinner Ella and Eli talked up the the next night's planned family party, assuming that he would join us as one of the family.

Lora pulled me away for a conference. "I don't *want* him at my birthday party," she confessed in a harsh whisper. "Is that bad of me?"

"It's *your* birthday. Invite who you want." I was pleased

for her to want the separation.

"I mean, just because *he* decided to show up doesn't mean *I* have to change my life around—does it?" She bit her lip. "Eli and Ella are going to flip out."

"They can invite him to *their* birthday parties."

"He didn't bother to *come* to Ella's party. God," she said, really mangling her lip, "this is hard. But I have a *right* not to have my ex-husband at my birthday party, right? I mean, I'll be giving him something to be non-attached about."

"It'll be good for him spiritually," I agreed.

We laughed, two conspirators for freedom.

Eli and Ella were summoned to join the conference. Not invite *Daddy* to Mommy's birthday party? Eli, keyed into the injustice and the hurt to Al's feelings, shouted, "You can't *do* that. It's not *fair*!" Ella stayed sullen, letting him handle it for her. But they had to admit, under the laws regulating birthday parties, that Lora could invite whomever she wanted.

Al didn't like it either. "I don't understand why we can't be friends," he complained mildly to Lora, hurt to be told so definitively that it wasn't his home any more. Looking really sad, he turned his attention to comforting his empathetic daughter Ella, weeping at his side, and to calming loyal son Eli, who, fists clenched, glared furiously at his mother.

It went against the grain to uninvite a guest, to shut out the kids' father, to be rude to the wayfarer, and we feared we might traumatize the kids forever or injure the solidarity and warmth we had built among ourselves.

But we learned something important that night. For when at last we put Eli and Ella, who had spent the evening glowering at us, to bed, they were cheerful and carefree. Alone in their room with us, they danced on their beds, sang songs, told stories of the day with clarity and energy. Somehow—by constructing a defining fence around our family?—we had made them quite happy.

After we kissed them good night and called their sad-eyed father for his turn at bedtime, Lora and I retired to her room for gleeful post-mortems with our limbs wrapped around each other. "One of your greatest moments," I told her. My lips were between her lips, my hand stroked her smooth flank. "You taught me a great lesson."

"Which is?" asked Lora, pleased to be praised.

"That the truth told clearly transforms the world."

"I did that?" She let her hand wander down to my thigh. "I

was pretty great, wasn't I?"

"You definitely were," I said seriously and, starting with her bare shoulder, I thanked all the parts of her. And while Lora and I made love, the children slumbered beside their father, who had fallen asleep while putting them to bed—that homeless one who had no place because of us and because of whom we had so much trouble knowing our place.

Al must also have understood Lora's revision of the guest list as a milestone in family building, for the next evening he made such a big production out of leaving before the party—huge sighs, martyred suggestions that he wasn't really over his stomach flu yet, even a tear or two—that Ella and Eli, encouraged, began to yell and weep all over again.

These cries of the children echo down the years of our lives.

As if by some signal Lora and I woke together in the nights to touch. I longed for her while I shot baskets with my 7th graders and wrote poems into which flowed the tastes and sounds of our time together. There was nothing I did not tell her, no ashamed desire I did not confess, no one with whom I had ever made myself so completely naked.

We went on vacation to the Redwood country, to bathe in private hot springs in the forest. Birds sang from the rocky ledges above us while Lora, in natural waters, wept for her life breaking apart in stages. Seeing her tears, I knew her grief as my own good fortune, as she gave up her old life and turned her face fully to me.

She whispered of suicide, imagining that we, too, might argue and separate. "No," I pleaded. "Even if we were to break up, I want the comfort of knowing you're in the world with me."

She looked so beautiful—her wet hair tied back, face open and amazed, droplets shining on her breasts and shoulders. Seized with power beyond myself, the poet at last in a place without words, I scooped up water in my hand and poured it over her head, like a sanctification. So we were priests to ourselves and made our private marriage.

Later, exploring in the woods, I heard her voice in my mind, calling to me, then returned to camp to learn she had been calling to me in her mind.

We lived, some days, a life of miracles.

On his next visit, Lora told Al she was giving up Rosen and changing her name back to Sachsman.

"What's the matter with Rosen?" Al asked.

Looking nervous but determined, a head of broccoli in her hand, Lora faced him in the kitchen doorway. She took a deep breath and told him the rest. "Also, I want to get a divorce."

"A divorce?" He looked a little blank. Then he sounded a little annoyed. "A *divorce*?" There was a long pause. From where I sat behind a book in the dining room, pretending not to be listening, I imagined him doing an internal meditation to detach himself from things of this world. "Fine," he said at last, more angry than detached. "You give me what I have to sign. But you take care of it. And I won't *pay* for it."

It was not his greatest moment, I thought. He came back into the dining room and went past me without looking or speaking. It was odd, I thought, how such an important thing got done in such a casual way, in a doorway, standing up.

I woke in the night saying her name. I turned and found her awake already beside me, waiting for me in the darkness.

We were doing pretty well. We had space and time to work, we knew passion and playfulness, and we had the makings of a family. And especially we were connected by the desire and the need to live our lives as artists—not only to do our work but to live a combination of wild invention and stern discipline and shape that into real life.

Against the wishes of the lady swami, Al took a girlfriend, a woman named Madrone (real name Barbara, from Tenafly, New Jersey). Finally, he left the ashram with her, and they went traveling, first cross-country west to east, then up and down the continent north and south to Guatemala and back, in a little van that Madrone bought out of the stipend she received from her father, a radiologist.

She was a space case, full of chatter about yogic levitation, herbal healings, unlikely governmental conspiracies. But she was pretty, with pale skin and wide blue eyes, and she was nice, even if impossible to take seriously. The kids liked her a lot.

Al and Madrone bought two goats in Oregon and moved, goats and all, to West Virginia, where Madrone would use her father's radioactive currency to buy a piece of land. They stopped off one more time to see Eli and Ella, who couldn't believe their good fortune in getting to escort goats on clothesline leashes across the pedestrian bridge over the freeway.

Why Al and Madrone had to buy the goats in Oregon and transport them across the country, sharing with them their little camper-back living quarters, was not clear. Al claimed they were particularly good goats and especially cheap.

The night before they left, Lora insisted with Al that they have a discussion. She had divorce papers for him to sign. And she wanted to talk to him about money. After long reflection, she had decided that Al ought to contribute to the support of the children he had fathered.

Al was surprised at first.

Then he was outraged. "You're getting *paid by the State* to support them," he cried, "so what are you complaining about? Nobody's paying me!"

They closeted themselves in Lora's room for an hour, and when they came out they had an agreement.

Fifteen dollars a month per child. Thirty bucks a month. Three hundred and sixty dollars each year for the care and protection of two children.

In the morning, with the goats bleating at the little window in the back of the van, Al and Madrone climbed into the cab and took off, waving.

It wasn't very much money, Lora acknowledged, but it was something. The important thing was that the children were safe and secure, not living on an ashram or traveling with goats to uncertain destinations. We might be poor, but we were getting the gift of raising them, the advantages of being a family.

So we found ways to get the children what they wanted and needed and were content that Al was far away. That was the bargain.

Eli began having nightmares almost every night of a particularly disconcerting kind. He would come staggering out of his room, screaming, gesticulating toward something he was hallucinating in his dream, yelling with great intensity phrases no one could understand except for obvious words like, "Daddy! Mommy!" His face in anguish, he pointed at the—at the—at the—Oh, look, O Mommy, oh the—Oh, Mommy, please—Oh, please, Daddy, oh, please help me—oh no!

All the while he was asleep. The nightmare did not wake him up, and we had to work hard to bring him out of it, to get him to the point where he would come back to himself and sob uncontrollably in Lora's or my arms, his thin body soaked in sweat, his face a feverish mask of fear or sorrow, his heart pounding so hard in his chest that his whole body quivered. But he could never articulate what he was seeing.

He tried to describe the dreams to us: swirling whirlpools of colors that were drawing him down, down into them, turning him into something much huger than himself, making him part of something too frightening for words. He couldn't be less abstract than that.

The nightmare became an almost nightly event, usually just before midnight, as Lora and I were preparing to go to bed ourselves. Each dream was as terrifying as the one before, and there was almost never any articulate word that Eli yelled, no clue to their content, except the repetition of "Mommy!" or "Daddy!"

"No significance," Mars, visiting, said drily one night after we finally got Eli, sweaty and trembling, back to sleep. "Doesn't mean a thing. It's just being Jewish and from New York that makes you think of underlying psychological causes."

"Yeah," said Lora heavily. "We're too subtle, that's our problem." Lora felt culpable. Her separating from Al, her casting him out of the family, her insisting on divorce—all that clearly was, she said, Eli's nightmare subject. She had imposed this pain on her son.

After many weeks, she finally made a decision. She asked around, got a recommendation to a psychotherapist and went. The psychotherapist supplied a name for Eli's bad dreams—"night terrors." He was, she said, signaling his trouble, and she instructed Lora to bring him to therapy, carrying him bodily if need be.

I said therapy for a kid seemed weird. But Lora, protecting her cub, disagreed. "There's something wrong," she said and signed on. She seemed sure of what she was doing, as if she had found and recognized the right medicine. Eli had to be coerced at first, but he went, and the night terrors gradually receded. Lora justifiably felt vindicated in her decision.

That was how we entered the world of psychotherapy, with its optimism and bright promises.

The kids grew strong and smart and feisty. Eli outdistanced nightmares and chewed cuffs and, possessed of the manic energies and enthusiasms of his father, by age ten was learning everything set in front of him so quickly we sometimes thought we could see his brain waves. Ella, plump and sexy at six, with dark eyes and a wilful mouth, outgrew her pudginess to become a slim, warm girl of seven and eight and nine, able to listen with real understanding to grown-up conversation, drinking it all in. I comforted their wounds, figured out good presents for their birthdays, helped them to read and write, to cope with bullies and bicycles. I applauded the talent shows they put on for us, taught them games, manners, skills and values—in short, did everything that fathers do for children and then stood back, tears in my eyes, to see how well they were growing. Their virtue was my reward—what else defines the pleasures of parenting?—and I felt happy to be, not just a poet, but something greater than that, shaper of the very flesh of the world.

Abner Minksy, *pater familias.*

But what happened to you and me, my Lora? What happened to our love? Sex was only our metaphor: Lora and I were matched for the perfect fit.

I know as well as you, educated reader, that Love is illusion. The lover gazes into his beloved's eyes and sees—himself. I had the need to be a protector and she called me hero. Olfactory symbolisms buried deep in the animal brain make the heart leap and the blood throb. It has been scientifically proven: Love is psychology; love is biology. Love is illusion.

Do you believe that?

Color, too, is a lie. Yes, scientists have proven the robin's eggshell and the rose are only reflections of vibrations not absorbed: We see the leftovers of the light and call it color. Do you really believe that?

Sex be my metaphor. I loved Lora, and that was why she felt so good. Our lovemaking was tender, or funny, or rough, but always it aimed at one thing: at going deeper and knowing more, as if making love was not a physical thing at all but a rigorous form of honesty we had invented for each other.

We spent hours in bed together laughing and talking and touching, happy just to be in that place, *there*, where the real prize is Seamlessness, Homecoming, a Change of Heart.

We opened to one another with a ferocious commitment to

no-restraint: there was nothing we would not request or confess or do, no game we wouldn't play. Sex be my metaphor: We had entered that garden of perfect healing where there is no shame.

Even strangers, corroborating our truth, smiled at us for no reason in the street, recognizing us as angels—beings of light, not base reflections.

We were in love, imprinted on one another like kittens in a litter, one being.

CHAPTER 9

Even at the beginning, we fought, of course—passion like ours has its cost. There was hardly a moment during the day when I did not think of her. How could any organism bear that without beginning to scream?

So we burned sometimes not only with passion but with a kind of terror, almost a hatred arose because of being so intruded on by the other. And since every moment and gesture had its special significance in our private mythic life, small misunderstandings or frustrations, problems in the smoothness of the fit (a gruff word, an unexpected decision by one of us to spend time alone), became metaphysical crises. *If it isn't perfect, it's no good.*

Insane with the possibility that love was a lie, or that love was a trap, we would throw food or dishes against the wall or scream, forgetting the children and the neighbors, or fight with our fists until the anger turned to sex, diverting us again into the quiet pool of our longing for each other.

But after we were done fighting, we saw through the bitter haze on the surface of the other's eye into the dear matched soul, and could forgive, not only on the surface but down through all the levels, making everything clean between us again. Our embrace would seal it and we would be whole, reconciled, starting all over.

Sex be my metaphor: Who else thinks about you all the time?

Yet as we became a stable family, Lora and I fought more. Without any lessening of our desperate passion for each other, my mate and I began to fight without forgiveness. It took me a long while to understand why this should be so.

After Judy left, we had redivided the house, giving Eli and Ella each a room of their own. I got a study, Lora and I shared a bedroom. Then where would her studio go?

The sheds behind the house, even if we ran water and electricity out to them, would be miserably cold and damp in winter. So we agreed that Lora would have the living room. That much was easy. But then, like two Talmudists, we stumbled over the definition of "living room."

Lora said living room meant the room itself plus the connecting foyer up to the bedroom doors plus the back service porch—a studio with legs like an octopus that made half the public space of our home her studio. I wanted her to have the living room only; it was the largest room in the house.

We fenced with tape measures, pacing off distances, and kept it up in a growing fury for weeks before we reached a limp compromise that gave her the living room *and* the service porch, but not the space between. We both felt cheated. There was no deep forgiveness this time, only agreement.

Restrictions, definitions, control, disputes over the very need to compromise—Is that where the darker pattern begins to emerge, a sharp thread that is not quite drawn back into the complex tapestry of our terrible love?

Is it possible that two people should meet in a great burst of light and only learn later that their meeting was a mere chance collision as they traveled in opposite directions? That this collision unfortunately left them tangled together like two dogs stuck fucking, trying painfully to pull apart?

Please God, not that. Let our lives have meaning, let our histories be a source of comfort to us, not merely a form of garbage.

Our battling had begun, perhaps, like all good fights between lovers, as a way to bring ourselves to new levels of excitement and closeness. But now we fought like cats and dogs—snarling, puffed up to frighten each other and camouflage our own fear, with the ambition to do harm. The children, bonded now to me as well as to her, turned frightened eyes to us. They had seen parents becoming enemies once in their lives before.

But we could not stop. Day after day stretched out without resolution or forgiveness, as if the thing we really wanted was to fight, as if there could never be an answer to the question, "What do you want?"

Lora, what did you want?

And why did it depend on saying no to me?

As we became permanently a family, I began to nest. "You're a nurturer," our ex-housemate Judy had told me in the jargon of the times, "you have a strong feminine component." Particularly attracted to kitchen life, I cooked meals, organized the cupboards, found pretty dishes in thrift shops and carried them proudly home.

Eli and Ella also liked new dishes, but Lora said we didn't need them or didn't have room for them. I did not notice for a long while how quickly the new plates and glasses got broken. Who could have predicted it?

Yet our life remained eccentric and exciting—we were artists living together as a family, the children no less than Lora and I. When Ella wanted her ears pierced and requested we do it ourselves, we numbed her ears with ice cubes and Dr. Minsky thrust a needle sterilized in flame through the flesh while we all sang at the top of our lungs, "For He's a Jolly Good Fellow"—Ella's idea of an anesthetic song.

When we took a trip to Los Angeles to hook up with Lora's parents, on a vacation to the West, we surprised Eli by making his eleventh birthday party on the shuttle flight. We brought aboard a secret cake and had the stewardess deliver it, with candles lit, right after the snack. The stewardess and even passengers in adjacent seats joined us in singing "Happy Birthday to You." Eli was so surprised and embarrassed that for about five minutes he kept gasping for breath like a fish.

When Ella got a vaginal yeast infection, Lora read somewhere that yogurt was a cure. I rushed out, bought quarts of plain yogurt and poured it into the bathtub, where Ella sat in it and fingered it into herself—medical history in the making.

Lora and I invented sex by note. Sitting demurely at the kitchen table or a luncheonette counter, we would write wild promises and fantasies to one another until we got ourselves so hot we had to rush somewhere to finish what we had started. Then we pioneered reconciliation by note. Too angry to speak, we sat beside each other and shared through writing and small pictures what our mouths could not confess.

Our lives in our house on the hill were rich, deep and full of charm.

Sweet scent in the night
Remember it
When I'm far away—

If I was going to be father to two kids, maybe I should prepare myself for a career. I wasn't going to be a playground director all my life. I began to consider the notion of going to graduate school. My parents, delighted, said they would pay school expenses.

But Lora objected. She said, "You could make more money just going out and getting a regular job." She suggested, "If you want to read books, go to the library." She asked bluntly, "What's in it for me?"

I said, "If you want us to have more money, go out and get a job yourself." I told her, "I'm thinking about the future now." I added, "We're having a conflict of values."

"We're having a conflict because you're making plans that are only good for you instead of considering all of us," she said.

How could she think I was only thinking of myself? "I *am* considering all of us," I shouted. "If you can't see that, then I feel sorry for you."

"Oh, you feel *sorry* for me, thanks a lot. Go fuck yourself, Abner."

And so on.

Beneath great anger is always grief. That evening she finally found and confessed the real cost to her of me going to grad school: "You'll get too far out in front of me," she wept. "I'm afraid I'll be left behind." Under everything, an ancient fear of abandonment.

"Maybe you want to go to school too," I suggested.

She looked at me and a little crooked smile grew on her face. "Maybe I do," she breathed.

So I went to grad school, and Lora finished her bachelor's degree in a program combining art and psychology. But when, finishing my Master's, I started to investigate teaching jobs, applying to colleges in the East and Midwest, Lora panicked. She didn't want to leave San Francisco.

But Lora, there are no teaching jobs in San Francisco.

We talked and yelled, arguing over who should have the power to determine our lives and how to change them, until a solid offer from Athens College in upstate New York pushed us into bitter silence. The Dean had written a heartwarming letter of praise for me and my poems. It seemed like a possible home.

Lora said no.

We talked and talked. Lora, finally calmed by friends and Eli's therapist, at last agreed to go. But she had conditions: She would not have to work, she would have a large studio separate from our living quarters, and if she did not like it after one year we would move back to San Francisco. Yes, Lora. Yes, Lora. Yes, Lora.

I wrote my letter of acceptance to the Dean. Then Lora

changed her mind. "I want another year in San Francisco," she said.

"How can you just change your mind like that?" I protested.

"I'm not changing my mind. I'm still willing to go, I just need another year *here*."

This time the talk talk talk soon devolved into yell yell yell, the battling a constant high whine like a dentist's drill, a shrill mosaic background to the continuing ordinary domesticity of our lives. The kids went to school, we made dinners together, did our chores as arranged, talked about other things. Yoked oxen, we were nonetheless pulling two ways at once. Surely we would have to break up.

Two things saved us. One was sex. The other was memory—our memory of miraculous events, angelic moments of pure communion. About to separate, we would end up weeping to think of sacrificing the past, to think it meant nothing, that after all we could be merely passing figures in each other's stories. For months on end we chose exhaustion over dissolution.

And what comes after exhaustion?

Marriage.

Yes! I loved this woman, after all, and her kids were my children. After three years of living with her, the poetry and terror of my extended adolescence had led me to this promontory from where I could see a future spread out before me of productive work and family. It was not the perfect Blakean ecstasy I had sailed out from New York to find—but I was not William Blake. This new plan had the benefits of adulthood: consistency, continuity, family love, faithful fulfillment of obligations already shouldered.

I could attain many of my goals, I thought, and even do some good—not throw Eli and Ella back into the whirlwind of another family destroyed, our hearts all broken. I wanted a *life*, not a hand-me-down, not a neo-hippie construct, but identifiable identities, planning for the future, children of my own. I wanted vector—direction as well as acceleration. Since I was still dirt poor, nobody could accuse me of selling out.

And how long, after all, could I go on introducing Lora as "my friend?"

Indeed, when I looked for ultimate causes, it seemed obvious that we fought and misunderstood each other precisely because we had not defined our relationship. Were we permanent partners or just boyfriend and girlfriend? Were we making decisions together based on a joint planned future, or were we just having a good time while it lasted?

Almost thirty years old, then, an adult at last, I would consciously combine the two noblest professions, poet and father, and make a life of solid value. I would accept my littleness and out of it make the ultimate romantic gesture: I would propose to my beloved.

We spent a sweet two hours sitting on the deck among the blackberries behind the house, nursing goblets of a particularly tasteful rosé. It was a healing kind of afternoon.

"I wish we had some sort of spiritual discipline in our lives," Lora said, "like *omming* before dinner or chanting Hare Krishna or getting saved. You know what I mean?" She screwed her face up into her Lily Tomlin look and crooked her finger at me like a witch. "Do *you* have a personal relationship with Jesus?"

I laughed, pleased at our synchronicities. For I too, contemplating marriage, had been thinking along these lines myself—something to elevate and nourish our household, to unify us as a family. "How about hand-holding and a moment of silence around the table before dinner?" I suggested.

"Nicely non-denominational and not oppressive," pronounced Lora, sipping her wine. "Let's do it." She looked away into a distance, and I thought I, too, could see the image she was looking at: our family centered, quiet, reverential around the table.

That evening at dinner, as we sat down and Eli immediately grabbed for the pot of noodles, Lora said, "Hold it a second. Abner and I are wanting to make a new rule—"

"Let's not call it a rule," I suggested.

Lora nodded agreement. "A ritual," she amended. "Just a thing we do before we eat. We're all," she said, putting on her explaining-to-the-children voice, "going to hold hands, make a kind of circle and just sit quietly for a minute before we eat, okay?"

Ella rolled her eyes at Eli.

"It's cool," said Eli, deciding to cooperate. And so, permitted by the children, we held hands around the table, then wolfed down our food.

"I liked it," Lora said later. I did too. It seemed a nice way to begin, made me feel a more solid person, less rushed and reactive, someone attached to higher things in the world than noodles and cheese.

On the second night, Ella started to Om. Omming in itself would have been okay, but she did it in a particularly loud, overdramatic way—being sardonic, making fun of us for holding hands.

"You don't need to be embarrassed by this," Lora suggested.

"Hey, Ella, would you just be quiet?" her brother asked nastily.

We were meanwhile holding hands around the table. By eye contact, Lora and agreed what to do: We held the circle another few seconds, then dropped our hands and fell on the food.

The next night Ella had a fight with Lora before dinner and refused to participate in hand-holding at the table. "I don't see why I have to do it if I don't feel like doing it," she announced.

"Hey, don't make a big deal," her brother instructed her, gaining points with the grownups. "Grow up, will you? You're always making a big deal out of everything."

"Shut up," Ella told him.

"Hey!" Lora said sharply. "Both of you be quiet now. This is what we do at the dinner table. If you want to join us, fine. If not, you don't have to stay for dinner."

Ella immediately got up from the table. "Thanks," she said. Eli asked, "You mean if we don't want to hold hands, we don't get dinner?"

Lora, giving Ella no energy, didn't answer him, just put her hands out, and we did a three-way circle, stretching around the square table.

The night after that, Ella came to dinner late, so that we had held hands and begun on the food before she arrived. "You could have waited a second," she complained, as if we hadn't waited quite a while for her and as if she hadn't been late on purpose. That was a fairly silent meal.

The next night, Ella came on time but didn't raise her hands out of her lap when the time came for hand-holding.

"Listen," Eli said at last into our dim silence, "can't we just forget about this? It's just a hassle."

Lora and I looked at each other across the table. She shrugged and I glared. I felt angry to have a decision we had made as heads of household abrogated by the whim of the children. "Well, I'll be disappointed," I said, remembering to express my own feelings rather than accuse anyone else.

"It's dumb," said Ella. "I just want to eat."

"I think it's cool to hold hands," said Eli, "but not if Ella makes it into a fight every night."

Lora shrugged helplessly again, and we sat for a while.

"I'm hungry," Ella said.

I realized they were waiting for me. I was the holdout. Somehow, the three of them, mother and children, had agreed to forgo the handholding before dinner.

Maybe they didn't need anything to remind them that they were a family. Maybe Lora couldn't stick to an arrangement. Maybe we were a child-driven, child-ridden family. Whatever it was, it made me mad and sad. But I didn't know anything I could do about it, if Lora wasn't going to side with me.

So I closed my eyes for a meditative moment, setting a good example, and when I was finished opened my eyes and said in a small voice, "Let's eat."

Eli immediately began to shovel a pyramid of noodles onto his plate with an almost mystical concentration, his eyes filled with love for every single noodle, not letting a single dropped one of them be forgotten on the tablecloth, spooning out more and more until Ella interrupted him with, "Could somebody else get something to eat, Eli? God!"

And that was the end of our reverential, elevated pre-dinner moment.

"How come you didn't insist?" I asked Lora later, still annoyed about it.

"There's no point to the whole thing if it's such a hassle," she said. "Do you mind?"

"Well, to tell you the truth, I do mind. I thought you and I had decided that was what we wanted."

"Well, why didn't *you* insist on it, then?" she asked back.

"Because you wimped out."

"I didn't 'wimp out.'"

"What do you call it then?"

She shrugged. "Going with the flow—isn't that what meditating's all about?"

We were revving up. "Maybe it's what meditating is all about, but it isn't what running a *family* is all about."

"*Really*? When did *you* get so knowledgeable about what running a family is all about?"

"Look," I said, trying to piece it back together, "we said we wanted to make a certain thing happen. Something that would have a cumulative effect—we have to do it for a while to see if it's worth doing. How could you just agree to forget it because Ella didn't feel like doing it any more?"

"What am I supposed to do, force her to hold my hand?"

"You're supposed to keep her from running things around here, as if she's the parent and you're the child."

"Don't *worry*—Ella doesn't *run* things around here."

Both our voices were getting ugly and—Oh, never mind, you get the idea. We stewed about it for a day and a half and then we made up. What else was there to do?

Mars, though now an Angeleno, still dressed like a San Franciscan in jeans and a plaid shirt. He came up on a weekend visit—odd to have him as a visitor where I had been his visitor before—and after dinner one night we went for a walk. I told him my litany of complaints, my list of goals and my plan.

"You're going to ask her to *marry* you?" The tone of his voice stays with me after all this time: not just surprise, but a note of horror, as if he knew something I didn't. "But you've been telling me what a drag your life has been, how you two argue all the time."

We walked up the hillside in the dusky light to where trees grew. The cool air felt good on my arms. "She's a difficult woman," I admitted, "but I love her, and the kids are my kids now. How can I throw that away? And what would I do? Go back on the singles trail? Start sniffing after women again to find a *different* one to set up housekeeping and have kids with? And anyway," I went on, attorney for the defense, "a lot of my misery I have to be bringing along in my own suitcase, right?—it can't just be all someone else's fault."

I didn't realize then that the idea that it was my fault—that peculiarly Jewish interpretation of history—was a *cause* of my suffering. Maybe Mars did, for he said nothing, letting me prattle on about my virtue. "I can't spend my whole life thinking I'll catch some better fish. This is what I have, and it's deep. I have real obligations to Lora and the kids. I have to look out for what's best for us, even if Lora isn't able to see it yet."

Mars thought about that so long that I finally prompted him, "So what do you think?"

He sighed and scratched his beard. "Well, you know I *like*

Lora—she's intelligent, she's funny, she's talented, she knows how to have a good time. But she's *very* demanding. And she never exactly knows what she wants, and she's very energetic and aggressive about it, which means she has to argue all the time."

"You don't have to tell *me* that. That's what I'm telling *you*."

"Right—I'm being careful, because you're my friend and she may be the woman you marry." He gave me a loving look. "But to tell you the truth, I don't *get* it. If it feels so bad now, why arrange to do it forever?"

"Because I love her. And because it's the right thing to do."

"So what can I say?" Mars asked, putting his hand up and turning to look at me for a long moment. "I think you're a good man, Abner," he told me gravely, as if he were saying goodbye. In his voice, I saw my swart ship sailing off over the horizon, heard a melody beautiful and sad. "I hope it works out great for you," Mars went on, "and I look forward to dancing at your wedding. What does Lora say?"

Lora, for whose hand I asked a few days later, did not say yes. But neither did Lora say no. Lora did not even say maybe. Bewilderingly, Lora said, "*But how can anybody make a decision like that*?"

CHAPTER 10

Worldly reader, you have no doubt immediately changed Lora's *cri de coeur* into something you can understand. Enlightened, sensitive individual that you are, you now believe that your translation represents what Lora meant—that she was expressing the difficulty of making so life-shaping a decision. You say, She meant to indicate how much there is to consider, since she will be committing not only her own life but the future of her two children as well. Yes, you will provide a liberal (in the best sense liberal) and humane explanation of Lora's words, and you will imagine that within certain tolerances you are accurate.

Sorry, you're wrong.

Lora was not describing the difficulties and pains involved in making her decision. I too thought she was saying that the decision was a hard one, or even that she preferred the status quo to any change. That would have been bad enough.

But Lora, as I began now to learn, was crying out a literal despair: She did not comprehend how a person can undertake to behave in a particular way at a future time.

For she went on to say, and I quote, "If there's one thing I've learned, it's that you can't make the future what you want it to be just by deciding what you want it to be."

Many a slip 'twixt the cup and the lip is I think the way a poet once put that same idea. "You're right, we're only human," Minsky agreed drily. "Nevertheless, I am making a proposal, and you must accept it or reject it." (Nothing personal, just business—one of my worst qualities.)

"And if you can't decide," I said weeks later, "I'm leaving."

More weeks passed. As if recapitulating Elizabeth Kubler Ross's stages of dying, Lora went through disbelief, anger, self-pity—only, being Lora, she went through them all at once and always returned to the same bemused plaint: "But how can I make a decision?—I don't see how I can decide."

We went into therapy then too, marriage counseling for the living-in-sin. Caught between fear of being abandoned and fear of being trapped, Lora also hurried to Eli's therapist for additional one-on-one sessions, but it didn't help. The therapists failed her finally by telling her she was just going to have to decide.

And I—I did not see as clearly as I should have, among all the trees, the foresty final truth of the matter.

The truth was that for Lora her current situation was the perfect situation. Wed at twenty, bred at twenty, she was a woman whose freedom had been curtailed early, and she was wistful about what she had missed. To be sure, she recognized that her children were a form of riches, and she did not envy her single friends, now nearing thirty, the humming of their bio-clocks, but her regret persisted, as if for an alternate universe in which she could have a family, a career and freedom too.

The name of that other universe: Abner Minsky.

With me—with the good me, who didn't press for anything—she had everything she wanted: a home, a father for her children, a lover and friend, no legal ties, state aid, a room of her own and time to be in it. In the light of final freedoms approaching as her kids grew up and she began to be included in shows and known in the local art scene, she dreamed of long days of painting bisected only by a spartan lunch: the monk-life of the artist.

I wanted something different: not merely freedom, ecstatic personal experience, and time to write, but a family, a name, a place in the world, a situation I could count on, children of my own. Yes, that especially, that without possibility of compromise: children of my own flesh. Lora, will you marry me?

She couldn't decide. Another child seemed an entrapment, and marriage did not necessarily seem a protection: She had already given herself to that fantasy once, chosen marriage, and then found herself abandoned.

So, although I needed to know, she could not decide.

I issued an ultimatum: You must choose by such and such a date, so that I can get on with my own life.

She could not decide.

The day came.

I did not want to go, but I knew I had to. Suitcase in hand, my life on the garbage heap, I walked out. Lora sobbed at the door.

What a soap opera!

I was halfway down the Bernal Heights steps (the freeway construction was gone now and landscaped to meld into the street scene) when: "Abner! Abner! Abner!"— Lora came flying down to land against the railing out of breath to tell me "Yes I will yes."

Just what I wanted, sort of. I could not tell if it was love or fear that had triumphed in Lora, but getting married was what I wanted, right? The process had left me feeling flattened, exhausted, exasperated, slightly ridiculous, but it led somewhere, even to happiness, perhaps. Having learned to live on little, I was pleased in the end.

So, while I report it as necessary history, that was not what made me crack, not what turned my head into a cruel instrument, not what made my hope leak out of me as from a split melon, not what paralyzed me with melancholia (as the poets call it), bound me in depression (as the psychologists say), or filled me with demons (in the words of the priests).

Nor did I crack under the strain of negotiating our compromises: Lora would remain Sachsman; we would have one child (last name Minsky); we would go to Athens in a year (the Dean said okay), where, stripped of Welfare, she would work part-time (they *were* her kids, after all); she would have a large studio near our house in Athens (we had no house in Athens yet, but I guaranteed), and of course—oh, of course and forever—we would continue strictly to share equally all household chores and childcare responsibilities.

We called these meek adjustments our marriage contract. It was the least I could hope for and the best I could do. And indeed, as Lora and I planned our wedding, a kind of bright calm settled over our lives, proof that we had made the right decision.

My parents, who had let a long silence pass on the line when I phoned to tell them Lora and I would marry, did not suggest again that I could do better than a divorcee with two children. Lora's parents, who had often lamented her choice of another reckless and unstable man with no "prospects," seemed genuinely pleased, or maybe just relieved. The families got along splendidly at the day-before dinner party we made to honor them, and our potluck wedding struck a happy compromise of seriousness, idiosyncrasy and fun. We seemed to have learned to cooperate, my betrothed and I.

We postponed till the summer plans for a honeymoon trip, with funds generated from wedding gifts, to the Pacific Northwest. But during the summer, my father suffered what seemed at first a stroke, then turned out to be the crab of cancer eating his mind—a brain tumor. Round-faced and quiet, he was dying in Brooklyn. There was money and time for only one journey—

"When you get married," Lora instructed me, "you have to separate yourself from your family."

Leave my father to die while I go on vacation? I canceled our honeymoon and went to New York, reminded again that my wife had one foot in an alien moral universe.

But that was not what made me crack.

Nor did I crack in any of our great arguments, though I suffered the painful loss of many hopes for peace and comfort. No doubt the huge battle that developed when Lora objected to my joining a Saturday morning writers' group ("Then who'll stay with Eli and Ella if I want to go out too?"), or the one about me wanting to take early morning walks ("Why should your alarm clock have to wake *me* up just because *you* want to go out early?"), or the one about why someone with her artistic temperament might still be expected to find and hold a job ("But what I want to do is *paint* all day, not work in an office")—no doubt all that prepared the soil for my ultimate collapse. Structural materials, even steel and concrete, do wear out after continual over-stress.

But none of those fights destroyed the bedrock of love between us. All couples fight, and though we fought bitterly, we recovered in those days, we still had good times together, we still fit together just the right way, still understood each other's depths. And every time we fought so deeply that the tuber of separation began to grow in our hearts, we could not bear it and would reconcile, breaking through each other's resistance. For a few days it might seem that anger had won its victory, but we always found the sorrow underneath when we contemplated the world without one another, and we would confess and weep.

And so, as we packed to leave for Athens and Lora said, looking around at all our stuff, "We really should get rid of a lot of this," and made a big pile of books and artifacts to throw away—every single one of them something of mine and not a single one of them anything of hers, even though she possessed three times as much materiel as I—

All right, it's hard to leave a place that has been comfortable and kind and go off into the unknown, and we were both on edge. We fought and made up, embracing the adventure together.

No, that was not the time I cracked for good.

I can pinpoint the moment at which my inner reality changed, when something finally happened to me that would not go away.

We lived in Athens by then, in a big old house that gave everyone a bedroom and me a little writing den. We turned the two-car garage into the "nearby studio" that Lora had written into our contract. I liked teaching and was good at it. Beyond our fence were acres of wooded hillside and past them was a state reservoir. It was an idyllic setting.

The kids were a pubescent twelve and eleven by then, horribly vulgar and noisy but good-looking, creative, intelligent and polite to other people. We were getting along as a family, too, having managed the adjustments of the move, and we had hope for the future.

To me, the essential clause of our marriage contract was the agreement to have a child. Isn't that what marriage is for, after all? It was nailed down: one kid. I could survive with almost nothing but I couldn't accept eternal death. One kid.

One morning in the spring semester, just before I left for school, Lora and I were standing in the "guest room," the one with the good wooden parquet floors and little French windows above the alcove that let in the sunlight. Though small, it was a charming room. We needed furniture for it, and I had just presented some ideas about how to furnish and decorate it so that it could easily become "the baby's room" in the future.

Lora was standing by the window, looking down into the back yard, so I could not see her face. She said carefully, "What would your response be if I said I wasn't sure I wanted to have a baby?"

I felt a sharp spear pierce my side. I suddenly remembered that I had not thought for a year or more about Cyna, who always protected me and kept me on track toward what was real. "But we agreed," I said, "before we got married that we would have a baby together."

She said, "But I'm not sure I want to."

And I said again, as the familiar tightness blossomed and took hold of me, "But that was what we agreed when we got married."

She gave a little shrug, her back still to me. Then she turned to face me. "Well," she explained slowly, "that was the agreement I made *then*."

That's it, folks—no big deal, only the future slammed shut on the past. Not just the future of child-bearing and fathering, but the future of every kind of trust. I recognized this juncture immediately as the destination toward which all our arguing had been leading us—every irrational jump in our conversations, every little torment of misunderstanding, every innocent illogic by which Lora had defended herself against my complaints when our agreements failed: "That was the agreement I made *then*."

Perfidy raised to the level of social principle. And I was married to it, had staked my life on it.

That was when I cracked. The liquid of trust, that lubricant, I watched it spill out of me onto the good wood floor. The golden sunlight dried it immediately, leaving the kind of stain that shows only at its edges at certain times of day. Otherwise, nothing looked different. Only, without that liquid to keep it ripe, my heart grew hard and bitter. Ah, poor heart indeed.

Of course, we fought for days and weeks, we found our first paid counselor in Athens, and we even worked it out: We stayed together and had a baby, Hannah, my one and only. But something had changed forever.

That week, the people we were renting our house from informed us they wanted it back for themselves and we would have to move. All we could find was a flat too cramped for us downtown—no more roomy old house with back yard and woods. My department chairman informed me apologetically but firmly that he needed me to teach freshman composition instead of poetry electives. Insurance rates went up, supermarket prices went up, we never had quite enough money, and Lora never seemed to be able to find the part-time job she had agreed to find, even before the baby came. (Maybe that was just the agreement she had made then.) I couldn't figure out what I was being punished for, but I knew my poet's tongue had been torn out, for there were no more songs left in me, and after that almost everything I did seemed like impossibly trying to find a way to lick the wound.

And though our baby, my beautiful Hannah, was born almost two years ago, every day since then has included trials of distrust and argument, and I often feel that I am screaming inside as I try to learn to be resigned to the life I have made for myself. Even when we do not yell, even when we have our occasional good time, my wife and I continue our deep fight, for it is an argument much deeper than any daily event, something our reality is now lined with, as a coat is lined, and we carry it with us no matter where we go.

Can my own tongue grow again and heal me? O Cyna, let me learn to sing to you again before I die.

Now I hear their voices outside, under my window. They are home. Though tempted to stay put, in the hope that some miracle will be done and I will disappear or get too small to be seen or that they will kindly forget me, I close my notebook and push back my chair. If I stay where I am and ignore their return, I will pay for my valor with Lora's lack of discretion: hours of argument will ensue.

So I rise and go to greet them—my family—at the door. On the way, I drop a packet of alphabet noodles into the soup.

CHAPTER 11

First up the stairs is Ella. At thirteen and a half, she has a sultry know-it-all look on a face still slightly rounded with baby fat. She is dressed, as is her custom, in a jeans jacket completely covered with message buttons advertising celebrities and states of mind. A denim hat, also button-covered, is cocked on her head at a saucy angle. In this era of unisex, she is able to be cocky and saucy at the same time. We hug.

Eli comes next, lugging boxes. At fifteen, his face is darkened with a hairy fuzz that is not quite shaveable; under the fuzz, teenage acne gives him a surly adolescent look. (Sultry and Surly, my teenage stepchildren.) Eli's smile is affable—he is glad to be home, glad to see me, even. We hug.

All this is normal enough, even if my smile is a bit crooked and my embraces are not overly warm (I do not insist on duration). I greet Lora by taking Hannah out of her arms, carrying her for my talisman. She is the one I am glad to see.

As we mill in the mouth of the kitchen, Lora and I are civil with one another in that grim way that married people have, which they can hide from others, or think they can. That is, we are pointedly (to us) ignoring each other. Thankfully, there is a lot of bustling, but the kitchen is (to me) still steamy with our argument.

Eli and Ella, who each went on their trip with a backpack plus a small carry-on bag, have returned with one additional huge suitcase, two cardboard cartons and a large drum case. They drop everything in the kitchen, blocking access to the living room, then climb over the barricade and pull some parts of it after them. Having thus, like dogs, left unmistakable traces in the two family rooms, they separate.

Eli heads for his own room, to lay claim to it again. He will first burst in, then become immediately tentative, approaching his treasures with suspicion, sniffing the air and eyeballing the turf for evidence that a grownup has invaded it in his absence.

Ella meanwhile has thrown her jeans jacket across the kitchen table and is telling her mother the gossip from the home of Al and Madrone, who have decided on an "open marriage," even though they are not married. Madrone has taken a lover recently, Ella tells her mother with breathless sophistication, daring her mother to criticize, and Al is sad. Under her jeans jacket, Ella wears a pink leotard; a pointy bra secures and draws attention to her new breasts. Her mouth is going a mile a minute with the juicy details.

This entertainment delights Lora in several ways at once. She is able to disapprove of Madrone while savoring Al's downfall while getting to be maternally self-righteous that her little ones have been exposed to these shenanigans.

"And then she gave Rob a key to the house, so he could come in whenever he wanted, and Daddy still didn't say anything."

"He's very mellow," Lora says drily.

Ella shrugs; her little breasts shrug with her. "I finally asked him if it made him feel *bad* for Madrone and Rob to be upstairs in her room while *he's* downstairs with me and Eli, but—"

"Why don't you shut up," growls Eli, returned from his inspection tour. "You don't have to blab all the time." He is jealous for his father's honor.

"It's none of your business," retorts his sister. "I'm talking to Mommy."

"Well, don't talk *about* me."

"Who's talking about *you*? God! Why don't you go and—bang your drum or something."

Home sweet home. Why am I still sitting in the room, pretending not to be listening? Because I'm lonely? Because I'm interested? Because I'm paralyzed?

"Well, they're back," Lora says tolerantly, not to me. Eli rolls his eyes, to show he is remaining cool despite his twitty little sister's provocations. Anyway, reminded of it by her, he's off into something else: "Let me show you my drum—it's so neat." He drags it back out of the living room, opens the case for Lora and me to admire. "Isn't it cool? It's a Ludwig. We got it unbelievably cheap. Isn't it neat? And guess what—Daddy thought it was going to cost at least eighty dollars but we got it for only thirty, so"—he digs into his jeans pocket and pulls out a crumpled $50 bill— "so Daddy said I could have the difference. Isn't that *cool*?"

He is very happy, as he should be. Lora too is pleased for him, even though the gift comes from Al. "He gave *me* fifty dollars too," Ella pipes up, not wanting Eli to be too far out in front.

They're a nice little family. They're cool. I used to be cool too, but not any more. He gave them each a $50 bill? Just to spend? It has been a long while since I had $50 just to go out and spend on my own whims. I spend my money supporting these kids—Al keeps his for occasional impressive gestures of generosity that cost him maybe $200 a year.

And he's their father, so he gets the credit and the title. Of their younger years all they remember is a dark-haired bearded man with them at important times, but they cannot—Ella has told me this—recall clearly if it was me or "Daddy." Thus he gets credit even for part of the time he wasn't there. In the album of their personal history, I am a fading photograph.

Eli is banging his drum, just as his sister suggested. "Will you shut up already?" Ella tells him.

Boomlay boom. Hannah has climbed off my lap and toddled over to bang on the drum too, and Eli is teaching her how. Senseless noise expands. "Stop it," Lora says finally.

"Can I take drum lessons, Mommy?"

"We'll talk about it tomorrow," Lora parries. "Just put it away for now, it's late." She gets up and fills a bowl with soup—my soup—from the crockpot on the counter, tears a hunk of bread off the loaf, grabs a spoon from the drawer and sits back down with it at the table. "There's soup, if you kids want it." She hunches over her bowl and begins to eat.

This is not the most gracious way of inviting your family to dinner, but I expect nothing more civilized. "Good soup," Lora says happily, slurping and chomping, meaning her words as an invitation to her children and, perhaps, as a small signal of peace to me. Eli goes over to take a smell. "Abner made it," Lora tells him.

"I'll have some," Ella decides.

"Grate some cheese in it, it's good that way." Having had the idea, Lora fetches the cheese and the grater. Eli tears off bread and takes a bowl of soup. And now Hannah wants some too, so I set her in her high chair, and Ella fills the bottom of Hannah's special Oscar the Grouch bowl with soup, explaining to Hannah that it has to cool, and gives her some bread to tide her over.

"Don't you want any, Abner?" Lora is definitely working to make peace.

But I don't want any. It's a thick soup and I don't like the taste. "No," I say in a voice careful to be merely informative. "I think I'll go and grade papers for a while." I pause.

"Welcome home, kids," I offer.

The four of them are sitting around the table: Lora and her children. They look up at me. "Thanks," says Eli, painting his I'm-cool grin on his face, "it's great to see you." The females, even Hannah, merely look briefly up at me as I escape.

Back in my small cell, I latch the door again. On one edge of my desk is a stack of sixty-six student papers for me to read and grade. I have not looked at even one.

On top of them, the crown of failure, is the manila envelope in which I received my poetry manuscript back in the mail today from a chapbook publisher in Minnesota. Inside is a note from an editor named Ms. Emily Miller.

It is a bland name, and the letter thanks me blandly for submitting my poems. There are several of them deserving of praise, Ms. Miller says, but she then feels required to tell me, quoting back to me mine own poesy as proof texts, that she finds overall that my use of idiosyncratic devices obscures rather than enhances the meaning of the poems.

Another disappointment, another arena in which I have no home. Perhaps, as a professional and an adult, I could learn to use her criticism to make better poetry.

But there is no way to apply what she says to the work itself; criticism is mainly useful to readers, rather than to writers. I am not being stubborn here. I am willing to stop being so idiosyncratic and obscuring, I do not refuse. But as I place her letter of rejection into my file of rejections, I reread last month's, from a lady editor at a university press in North Carolina.

My Southern Ms. Miller regrets to tell me that, except for a few—and here she names the very ones which were unsalvageable in the view of the Northern Ms. Miller—she found my poems poetically rather obvious and over-directed, with too much thrust.

I have no idea what she means, beyond several specific fantasies of tying her to a bed and demonstrating to her too much thrust. When I showed the letter to Fred Petrucelli, a skinny Wordsworth scholar from New Jersey who is my office mate at Athens College, he startled me by suddenly leaping up to storm around our small space. It turns out he got three letters in a row last year from lady editors of quarterlies telling him his short stories lacked "narrative thrust." "These literary schoolgirls, with their degrees and their three-to-five of experience—voluntary prison sentences!—they sit on their genitals all day and write letters to authors complaining, 'You didn't make me come. I'm not *finished.* More thrust!' That's what these letters are about," he cried, throwing himself down into his chair again. "These women have got us by the literary short hairs." I would have gone out for a beer with him between classes to talk about it more, but I had too many papers to grade.

In the great American career race, I am far behind.

I used to revel in the fact that I had no career. I was free of that dullness with which others clothe their naked lives. Money may have reckoned most of the souls of America, but I was Whitmanesque, with nothing to hide, ready with my barbaric yawp.

Even poetry was not my career. No, I was too cagey to get caught. I wrote poems, that's what I did for the joy of it, that was my cover story, but I attached no career ambitions to it. Publishing is not the beeswax of poets, said Fat Emily, and I took her saying to heart. The business of poets is to keep close watch over small and essential details, to derive general meaning from isolated events, to be the antennae of the race, to sing and to avoid, in the great battle of life, the bullets and bombs of dull irrelevancy.

Yes, to survive is everything. I thought I had escaped because I did not make of noble poesy an ax with which to fell the tree of a career. I was wrong there too—another mistake. I may have no career, but I still have a job and must spend my hours grading freshman compositions.

O dull minds! O murdered prose! This has become my career and leaves me little inclination to write poems, and the ones I write are obvious to some and obscure to others.

Other poets—I know a few—reap publication, local fame and admiring glances. They inhabit their own small worlds in comfort, smelling of pipe smoke and pine chips, while I live out my travesty of family life in a cramped apartment and spend my days editing grammatical errors out of student sentences. What is writ large in my hand is the immortal phrase, "Comma splice!"

Every morning I stand paunchily before my congregation of witless adolescents, boring them with what they do not want to learn: how to explore a subject, how to make articulate distinctions, how to tell the truth or an entertaining lie. The amazing thing is that these nineteen-year-olds act hardly any different from my stepchildren: They too are insolent, calculating, opportunistic, lazy and devious. They act as if I am their parent—as if I care about them.

And most of them drive nicer cars than I.

As I sit staring at the stack of student papers, pounding, discordant music suddenly shatters the air and vibrates the furniture. Two separate screams of electric guitars and drums, hardly muted by the doors in between, grow louder in discrete increments. The children have returned to their rooms and are now having a music war.

It's too much. A person cannot think or concentrate in this huge barrel of noise. I have asked them many times to keep their record players down. I have asked nicely.

I suppose their intention is at least partly to intrude, and they have succeeded, since I am now paying attention to them, thinking about them, beaming hateful and dangerous thoughts at them through the all-encompassing lava flow of the sound.

I know that teenagers are not normal people. These two, for example, have no desks in their rooms, at their request. They do their homework lying in their beds with the music turned up threateningly loud. Both of them claim to be unable to concentrate unless this music is blasting.

That is a humorous detail, I know. I am not amused.

I know the whole routine. Asked to turn their music down, they complain that they are trying to do their homework or read. (Do I want to keep them from those benign and civilized occupations, after all?) However, since their rooms share a wall, the musical pleasure of one of them necessarily interferes with the musical pleasure of the other. Then each one turns the volume up a little more in order to hear without interference.

I can make out the next stage developing outside my door now. The music is blasting through all the rooms of our home, but neither of them is satisfied. Now they are banging on the wall in between, now they are screaming at each other. The electronic volcano gets abruptly louder as they spill with their dispute out into the living room, leaving their doors open, demanding justice from Lora.

I already know the scenario so well that I do not need to participate. I have already put in my time pleading; I have put in my time yelling; I have put in my time reasoning. I no longer argue about these things, because I know the response.

Sullenly, grudgingly, they will both turn the volume controls of their sound systems imperceptibly to the left. There, each of them will say, I've made the music lower. That is my hard-won victory—but the music will still be ear-splitting. It still is, though they have gone back in their rooms and closed their doors.

This time, however, I am ready. I have prepared. One afternoon while they were visiting Daddy, I did a little experimenting to discover which of the circuit breakers controls the electricity in their rooms. Tonight I will not be treated like an uppity janitor or grumpy comic policeman. Unable to think or to hear my heart's voice in the raucous shrieking of their music, I rise from my desk and open my door.

The music assaults me. Passing through the living room, I nod to Lora, who is reading—I should say shouting—a book to Hannah. A cozy domestic scene. Neither of them seems bothered by the noise. In the kitchen, I open the fuse cabinet. I am carrying around inside me a wonderful silence as I go, like a spy or master criminal. Little joyful throbbings erupt in my chest and throat as I flick the two switches.

At once the two teenage musics disappear. His, which sounds like repetitive rhythmic blackboard scrapings, ends very abruptly—he is listening to a tape; but hers, a dead-voiced punk band, gives a screech, dying with a dying fall as the needle digs in.

Elected silence, sing to me.

The kitchen, in which I am standing, is hooked into the same circuits as their bedrooms and has also been plunged into darkness. I experience all the pleasures of sensory deprivation.

In the second or two before the two of them find their voices and their doors and come tumbling and squawking out of their rooms, I feel I have struck a sturdy blow for my own freedom. Power is in the ability to act, and I have acted. I am a freedom fighter—an Afghan, protecting my harmonious pre-modern culture against the depredations of the uncaring machine people. I am a Maccabee—

Now they spring from their rooms. I hear them in the living room, where Lora, after a moment's pause, has continued to read to Hannah: "The lights went out! What happened?"

"You increased the volume of your record players so much that the fuse blew," I tell them, strolling back into lighted space.

"Really?" asks the girl, impressed by the power of adolescence, but the boy narrows his eyes at me. For a moment he isn't sure, then he knows he is being tricked. He marches past me into the kitchen. "Is there a candle anywhere?" his annoyed voice comes back, and I hear him fiddling with the switches; click/click—the lights go back on; heavy metal and the first slash of Lady Punk jar the plaster, as the boy, a young bull, stamps back into the living room to confront me.

Can you understand how noisy this all is? They are screaming murderously, complaining above the sound of their horrid music, which they now refuse to shut off. Their faces are angry and bitter against me.

I, however, am quiet inside myself. I hear them. I hear my wife yelling now at them that if they want to stand out here and talk about this they had goddamn better well turn down their record players (to which Eli petulantly replies, "I don't have a record player—how come you can never remember I have a *tape deck*?")—but I am quiet inside. I have the internal good will, the equanimity and moral strength that comes from being a freedom fighter, doing the holy work. I am someone who will not break even when captured and tormented.

"Why don't you at least talk to them, tell them what you want, instead of shutting off the fucking lights all of a sudden?" Lora yells at me.

"If my record is scratched, you're gonna get me a new one," my stepdaughter tells me, breathing hard, eyes flashing.

It doesn't matter to me. I have perfect faith that the oppressors can win no permanent victory over me, for I am far away where none of them can reach, in a landscape of my own devising, where I wait for my only true collaborator, my Cyna, to find me. I know I am trapped, but perhaps she will show me a way out.

"Please turn your music down, children," I instruct them in a deadly voice, doing my wife's will. Though furious, they obey; I will have a small while of relative quiet.

I turn and go back into my small study. I lock the door.

Eli and Ella were finally asleep, I had tucked and googled Hannah until she too had fallen into that thick dormancy to which small children go, and then I had returned to my office to grade papers. Soon I heard Lora's footsteps outside my door, and then her knock.

"Can I please talk to you?" she said in a small voice.

I went out to her and sat in a chair across from her in our living room.

Lora's current paintings are of naked men and women being sold, brutalized or betrayed. She means them as social commentary and speaks articulately about her intention to comment on our culture's inability to distinguish advertising from pornography, sex from violence, the message of art from that of movies and television. Yes, the ceremony of innocence is drowned. Lora's work is powerful indeed, but I think of it not as works of art so much as assaults. She insists on hanging two of the largest of this series, one naked male and one naked female with labia exposed, in our living room. I have confided to my wife that they are not the sort of thing I want to look at all my waking moments, raise children among or have on the walls no matter who is coming for tea.

Lora sees the matter differently. "This is what I paint," she says, "this is my work. I ought to be able to hang my own art in my own house. Why are you so damn uptight?"

I took the chair that lets me keep my back to the paintings.

She said, "Abner, I can't stand this any more. I know I've been feeling bad lately, and maybe not acting all that nice, and maybe my vision of it is all off—but I don't think so. You don't want to touch me. You don't want to spend time with me. You leave early to go to work, then you stay away all day, then you come home and we have dinner together, but you don't even want to talk with me. You talk to Hannah more than you talk to me. Half of what you want to talk to me about is her.

"I don't know what to do. And then you stay up late reading or whatever, sitting in your office—thinking, you say—and half the time you fall asleep in there and don't come to bed until the middle of the night. Maybe that's okay, maybe it doesn't mean that you don't care about me, but I need more than that, I want more than that—"

By now what had started slowly, with some modulation, had gained momentum and was rushing out of her (as I had many times before heard it come rushing out of her), and while she spoke I had my own rushing series of responses.

First, that she was right, she needed more and deserved more. But more important, that I needed to choose a response that would give me what I wanted, so that I had to first decide what it was that I wanted out of this conversation that had been forced on me. And while I tried to do that, the great sadness of it washed over me: that after all these years together what it had come to, came to often, was my wife's small-voiced pleading for me to pay attention to her, and my hard-hearted lack of interest.

But what did I want now? My first ambition, because I no longer felt any hope that we could accomplish real change, was to invent an answer that would not prolong the conversation—because my true immediate ambition, I realized abruptly, was to get back to my office.

And—O hollow truth—deeper than that callow feeling of merely wanting to end the trouble by ending the conversation was: nothing. My sole ambition was to provide the answer that would cause me the least problem and waste the least time.

And that answer, I know always, is "I love you."

Not to say, "You act a way that makes me hide from you; you are full of small and large deceptions, therefore I do not count on you; you disagree with whatever I say, therefore I do not talk to you; I raised your fucking kids for you and your thank-you has been to say, 'Do more and don't expect anything in return.'"

Because then would come her yelling and my yelling, her defenses and my accusations, and we would have the usual big blow-out, followed by silent fury for many hours or days, followed by tender gestures of false making up.

I wasn't up for any of it. I had papers to grade, and I was glad to avoid the costly payments before the making-up.

So—as calculating in romance as a European but never as smart—I reached my hand out to Lora and confessed how right she was. Doesn't a wife deserve better than this distant manipulation from her man, this empty shell of relationship? Doesn't a woman have a right to more than the mess of a marriage gone bad, locked inside it for reasons of history, fear, convenience and the last tragic flickerings of love? My false heart wrenched in pain for a moment to realize that she loved me, that she had waited through these long months and years of my deep disappointment in her while hoping for things to work out well.

I held her hand, I stroked her arm, I spoke soft words: "I love you, Lora. I do want it to be better between us." Meaning it even while I pretended, watching the beginnings of her sorrow overflow as tears, I steeled myself against the tender remorse that threatened to well up inside me too, knowing by now that it would lead nowhere. Giving in, we would inflate it together into a bubble of sexual illusion, we would get horny and fuck, somehow believing in our bed that something could, after all, change. But once I came, once the bubble popped, I would know that nothing was really different, that we had merely pasted it poorly back together for the night or a few days more.

I knew, in short, that nothing would change from believing that something could change.

And all the while I sweetly held Lora's hand, I was wondering how I could escape.

But something must have been revealed in my face, try though I did to make my eyes soulful, for Lora squinted through her tears at me with a concern I could not match. "What is the matter, Abner?" she asked. "Don't you realize that you have what a lot of other people are dying to have? A wife who loves you, two beautiful stepchildren, a daughter of your own. You have a family, a family that cares about you. Why do you want to throw that away? You want to throw it away, don't you?"

And though she began to weep again out of her own unhappiness, there was an edge of bitterness in it too. "You're a sick person, Abner," she said.

Yes, I thought as I fought against my own tears welling up to hear the truth of what I had turned my back on, yes, you're right, I'm sick. I had begun to be used to this horrid tightness in my chest and eyes, as if it was simply the normal way men live, as if all the symptoms of my rage and grief were not symptoms at all but merely elemental facts about myself, merely the way I was.

I could not even tell myself at that moment what I was so unhappy about. All I knew was that I would not cry and I would not yell and I would not—this most of all—I was not going to tell the truth.

"You're right," I said. "I'm a sick person. I'm a sick person because I'm tired of your goddamn kids." It was, I saw in horror, going to all come spilling out, as if I had not just now vowed to myself to hold it all back, be self-sufficient as a stone. "Yeah, sure," I heard my voice say, "I'm a sick person because I'm tired of having nothing that's my own and because I'm tired of you expecting me to play father to your kids and half the time mother too, and because I'm tired of not getting anything back for what I've given you and them. You're right, I'm sick of it. I'm not interested any more in doing what's good for Eli. And I'm not interested any more in doing what's good for Ella. I've already spent years of my life putting their needs ahead of my own. Fuck them, Lora! I'm sick of being ripped off. I have some needs and rights in the world too, and I've already given up plenty, sacrificed plenty, to give your kids what you and they thought they needed—"

"And you."

"And me what?" I barked, not understanding.

"And giving them what *you* thought they needed." She meant to remind me of my choice of deep involvement with them, but I wasn't buying it.

"Right, giving them what I thought they needed. Now it's time for them to start repaying the debt. It's time for them—your fucking kids!—to start to understand that I am not their father but an incredibly kind stranger who has for years given and given and given and given—. No more. No more, Lora. That's it!"

I am a madman. But even now, raging around the room in a frenzy, I worry that I will wake up Eli and Ella, will inconsiderately interrupt their sleep and be humiliated to be discovered fighting like a lunatic with their mother. Yes, I am a truly crazy person.

But the yelling, to which I had promised myself I would not surrender and which therefore represents yet another failure of my soft will, feels so good to me. I could rail for hours and not be done.

This is the confrontation toward which Lora and I have been building all day—for days. It has begun.

. . . . I feel as if I have blacked out for a while. When I come to, Lora and I are shouting at each other. In that watery dark place where I went to escape my life, my life has passed in fragments before my eyes. I am drowning in disconnected events, full-color portraits of old hurts and disappointments. That is all I have left of what used to be a rich inner life.

Now I have returned from it, and Lora and I are shouting at each other.

"Don't you see," she cries, "underneath all your anger it's because you care for them so much. Why do you want to deny that? Why do you want to give that up?"

"I don't want to care about them. I get nothing back for caring about them. They aren't my children, and you have made it so that they won't listen to me at all. You think it's some sort of great compliment that they treat me as badly as they might if I were their father—and then they go you one better and treat me worse. What is it all for, for *me*? What am I supposed to be *getting* out of it?"

"A relationship with them! You raised them. You loved them and you told them you would be there for them, that you would be their protector and their parent. And now you're selling them out. You're *lying* to them! You complain that Eli doesn't keep his agreements, but he's only fifteen years old and the complaints you have against him are only about what time he comes home at night. But *you*—you've lied to them about being their father!"

He lied to me about being my son, I want to scream back, but my mouth is filled with sobs I have to restrain, and my eyes are filled with hot tears, and my insides are raw with adrenalin and with bile—raw with feelings I can't sort out. I don't scream the words that come to my mouth; I don't even know what I mean by them: How could he have lied to me about being my son?—it doesn't make sense. He is pursuing his proper project, which is getting himself independent and going off into his own life. Am I so stupid that I call that a betrayal? What do I want, for him to sit on my lap?

The truth is that I don't know what I want, yet I know there is something I want that I cannot have. I want this young man to be my own flesh and blood, my own real son, not split in his loyalties between his "real" father and me. I want that, I cannot have it, and this fills me with such a fury that I want nothing at all, want them to get out of my sight and out of my life, be blotted into nothing. Let me alone, I scream in my silent insides, just as I did when I was a fat little boy and my big brother would trick me and then mock me for my tears.

But Lora does not know how to leave me alone. This is her worst quality and her most noble. She sits there, watching whatever it is my face has become as I project on the screen of my features the almost impossible-to-bear confusion that my life has become. The anger has gone out of her face and when she speaks her voice is soft and caring.

"If only you knew how much they love you," she tells me, wrenching tears from me, so that I turn my face halfway away from her, "and how much they need you."

She doesn't realize that the word "need" hardens my heart: I do not want to be needed, it is the needs of these three people that have gotten me into the trouble I am in now—my insane, my maniacal, stupid need and desire to fill their needs, to take care of them. (I tried once to negotiate this with Lora, claiming the right to some reward from her for everything I had done for her kids—packed their bags for trips, paid for their dentist bills, cleaned their rooms, loved them—everything. Lora did not agree. "We all had our needs," she instructed me. "You needed to give, maybe Eli and Ella and I needed to take. I don't think that gives you any mortgage on anything. I think we're even.")

They need me? Fuck them. Let them take their needs and go swimming with them in shark-infested waters, let the water turn red with their bloody needs—don't tell me about their needs, Lora. I have needs too, and I don't see anybody exactly wearing themselves out to make sure I get them fulfilled. Get yourself a new boy because I am done eating shit in order to satisfy all of your needs.

And who even knows if it's true? All at once my mind goes clear for an instant, and I realize that I am being manipulated anew. Do they need me? Who says they do? Why, it's Little Bo Peep herself, assuring me that her sheep nee-eee-eed me.

I am standing in the middle of the living room and my tears are leaking out of my eyes and running down my fat face into my beard, because I am filled, as I am always filled these days, with anger and remorse and guilt and shame and longing for what I can't have and can't even clearly name. But for a moment I manage an inside view of my little drama and can identify one of Lora's most basic manipulations: her insistence on the family constellation in which I become the Good Al, take his role, raise his children, support his children, supply his children's needs, as if that is what I was born into the world to do.

But whose needs am I filling?

These kids don't need me; let's start with that proposition. They have a father, and their father, having come back into their life, now wants to get to know them, buy them expensive gifts, send them money to spend, fly them south for the summer and holidays. Think about it, you lummox Abner Minsky, impresario of your private Follies: These kids may *not* need you. Give up your guilt, throw away your crutches and walk. These two children have no more need of you. They used to need you, perhaps, they certainly used what you gave, but now they have sucked you dry, there is nothing left to feed on, and they have gone on to the next stage in their life cycle.

Yes, the evidence points to it. Why is this fifteen-year-old bastard so insolent: because he needs you? Why, when you ask her to sweep the kitchen floor, does this twit of a thirteen-year-old twat run off to her friend's house and not let anybody know where she is all night, so that you are up all night in a panic? Because she needs you? It isn't, as a logical proposition, very likely, is it? Who needs you, then? And who needs you to believe that it is these two children who need you? To whose benefit is this huge hustle?

Why, the Little Woman. Yes, she needs you to believe with her in the delusion that Bad Al can be written out of the script, that there never was the first marriage, that our family unit is not a broken vessel.

O Minsky, you have been taken for a ride.

All this strikes me in a moment and makes me calm: no more tears now, no more confusion. I peer into those hungry eyes, that needy face that wants nothing more than to bestow its love on me, to help me through my difficulty until I see how much richness there is for me in her children's needs, and my eyes fill with venom like the two teeth of a snake. I breathe in, I breathe out, returning to the center of myself. I notice details around me, the frayed armrest of our second-hand sofa, the chewed apple core that Eli left on the edge of the bookshelf, the baggy front of Lora's Bozo-the-Lesbian-Clown overalls. "You talk about need," I say in a quiet voice, "but what if I don't need *them*? Just because they have a need doesn't mean that I'm supposed to fill it."

Only a minute has passed, a minute and a half, two minutes, but I feel as if I have gone on a long journey and returned. My heart is a cruel instrument, no less than it was before. No healing has happened except that, for one moment, the curtain of guilt has parted and I have seen the bright possibility of not acting on behalf of the others but merely doing what I want—acting for myself, like they do. I could be a poet again, the instrument of my own salvation.

"Yes," I say again, "what if I don't need *them*?" For one precious minute I am free, my own boss again. And that might be a cause for rejoicing, if I were not, at the same time, still filled and vibrating so with anger.

"Then what do you need? What do you want? Is it only to hate us all forever?" Lora's voice is shrill with her own pain. "Abner—is what you want to leave? Is that what you want? I listen to you and I don't hear anything else. Is that what you need—to go away? Just say it, if that's it. You bastard, just say it!" And when I still say nothing, she cries out, in a voice I have never heard from her before, a rasping cruelty in her throat, as if she is doing damage to herself: "Go already. *Get out*! JUST GO! Do you think I want to be your jailer?"

. . . . It is not as if I have not thought of it before. But just at the moment when I wish for nothing else, just then that old, awful flood of tenderness rises up in my chest, tidal, that deep knowledge of how much Lora and I have shared and how much I would be giving up, that foolish desire to be tricked again and again in the hope that maybe it could work out this time. All the deep hatred and love I feel for Lora expands until it makes a sound inside me like the beginning of a baby's crying. The great crystal of my life with Lora—ten years of moments squeezed into a huge ball—hangs before me, a thousand refracted images pass before my eyes. Shall I grasp it now at last and throw it away?

Not that I would get to escape so easily. All the fleshy crevices of my fucked-up union with Lora Sachsman would secrete their fluids into our lives while we worked things out. There would be so much to work out—we have a family and a complicated life together. And how can I even think of leaving my Hannah behind in this woman's household to be made crazy like her?

But the whisper of freedom is luscious in my ear. I want to go, let go, transform myself—to give it all up and start a new life. It is what I want most, just to get out, to be free of this hard and rocky soil that my life has become and start over somewhere else.

Man alone is that creature who cannot escape suffering by flight, says Dr. Williams.

But he's wrong.

Ask Gauguin. Ask Mars. Sometimes—some places—it just doesn't work out for a man. Ask the Jews. Some places and sometimes you can start over again. Sometimes you make a big fat fucking mistake (a *fucking* mistake) and the thing you need to do, the very and only thing you must do, is get out.

Am I a tree that I have to stay where I am no matter what the weather? Not escape suffering by flight? Tell the starving Africans that. Tell the prisoners in the penitentiaries that. Tell me that, living in a world I *made*.

Get out, man. Get out.

PART TWO

JOURNEY AND RETURN

CHAPTER 12

Summertime.

I have hugged them goodbye indoors and then again, lingeringly, on the sidewalk. Now I wave to them waving goodbye to me: a family tableau. Lora carries Hannah in her arms. Hannah is also waving goodbye. Ella's face seems sullen, but that is the adolescent look—who knows what she is thinking? Eli stands gawky, tottling in a small circle on stiff legs like a pelican; the poet's eye catches him ill at ease, not knowing how to be cool or even if being cool is the cool thing to do in this circumstance. Biological father left long ago, and now another father may be slipping away.

The underplate of the station wagon scrapes on the driveway, and I redirect my attention to wheeling backward into the street. I recognize this as the true first moment of my new life, as I remove my attention from my family and begin to concentrate on myself.

We have talked about this. O boy, have we talked about it. Lora and I talked about it all the time. Lora and I and Mrs. K. talked about it an hour a week for the last two months. Lora and Eli and Ella and I all talked about it together. I talked about it separately with Eli and with Ella, taking walks with them to explain and to reassure them that none of what was happening between their Mom and me was their fault or responsibility.

Ella cried. Then she talked about the time we had almost collided with a deer on a dark road and barely missed, as we skidded across lanes onto the shoulder, both the deer as it leapt away and a telephone pole. "I didn't tell you why I cried then," she said.

"You said you were scared."

"I was afraid I was going to die without you and me ever being friends again," she confessed. Her eyes brimmed over.

"We *are* friends," I assured her, not sure if it was any longer the truth. I felt moved but distant. Ah, Minsky, connoissieur of emotional scenes!

Eli, as much my son as his father's, was even more straightforward. "I'm doing pretty great in my life," he told me with a confident grin. We were standing in front of our house, preparing to go in after our final walk-and-talk. "I mean, I know I owe you a lot for making me who I am. I mean—I just wanted to thank you for being my stepfather and raising me and everything." It was a nice speech, impressive for the difficulty of a boy his age to say such things. I hugged him, knowing that behind his gawky bravado were worries he could not confess: What next? Does step-parental love continue after divorce, if it came to that? Would we be friends again? I was moved by him, too, I cared for him—but I did not forget that he too, like Ella, also had sensible private motives for reminding me of our joint history.

And so, refusing to become entangled again in history, I promised Eli, as I had promised Ella, nothing.

In less telling ways, I talked with everyone else I knew, finding out what I thought about what I was doing by how I explained it to others and by how they reacted. Lora talked about it with most of the same people and constellations of people as I did, plus she ran it through the press of her much wider social grid—the feminists, the social workers, the artists, the academics. It went out on the wire and came back translated to me through her, so that one day she admired me as someone really trying to change my life, while another I was oppressing her by taking off on my own and leaving her with the kids. (Some days, of course, merely being her husband was oppression of womanhood enough).

With each other, Lora and I ran the gamut of all that Lora and I knew how to do—be furious, be funny, be curious, be up-for-anything, be loving, be full of sorrow, be protective of ourselves and each other, not give a shit anymore. In the end, we worked out a cover story we could believe: that I didn't completely know *what* I was doing, but that I was going off for the summer to find out. We were relieved to find a label for it: This summer is "Abner's vacation."

Maybe, Lora and I admitted to each other, we were divorcing. Maybe we were learning that we couldn't live without each other. Maybe the two things weren't even mutually exclusive. Nothing permanent was being decided, we said.

We hoped that was easy for Eli and Ella to understand. Maybe it was no big deal, just summertime. After all, the deepest knowledge of the young is that summers are free time. So Eli and Ella are flying down to West Virginia to be with Al and Madrone. While Abner is off on his own for a while, Lora will have a scaled-down household with Hannah, on vacation from the rest of us.

None of us knows what to think, really.

I am going away.

I look down the familiar street of frame houses and tidy front yards shaded by oaks and maples. Our crowded flat fills the second floor of one of these houses, I have seen this view a thousand times. Yet for a moment, it all looks new to me, as it did on our first day here, when this handsome, sturdy town, tucked into hill and lake country in upstate New York, made us feel we had come to live in a picture book.

Yes, this is a lovely town.

What am I doing? How could I leave these people with whom I am so bound up? How could I leave my own sweet child?

But how could I stay? Can I be trapped forever? It is the death of Cyna to stay, it is the smallest, necessary goodness to myself to go. As Mars says, Sometimes it is a kindness to send people on their way.

Yes, I am glad to be leaving.

With a final wave, I peel away from the curb. The car window is open to blow the sweet June air back into my mouth. I navigate the familiar streets to the highway, and soon I am traveling east at sixty miles an hour in the pursuit of happiness.

Even last night, we fought, screamed the old recriminations at each other, incapable of playing nice even for the sake of our last night together, while the kids retreated to their rooms.

"I took care of your kids all these years as if *I* was their mother, and you—"

"And all those times *you* stopped talking to me for days at a time, and I—"

"And you prepared my dinner and then *apologized* to Eli for it, as if—"

"And when we were only living together and you told me you would *never* marry me. And when I had the abortion, you took me there but wouldn't speak to me. And all those times you let me go to Welfare by myself, even though you were living off that money too, and—"

"*I was not*. I *had* a job—"

"And I *bore your child* but that's nothing to you—"

Every accusation against me was true—I had committed all these wrongs. I had been sullen, stopped talking, separated myself from her pain, patronized her, acted with contempt, allowed an abortion but not forgiven her for it—I had milked the cow and complained about the milk. It was all true, and yet it was not truth.

And after I had yelled myself dry, I fell asleep at my desk, unable to manage any conciliatory gesture, my head cradled on the pillow of my arms, my bones jammed in the chair. When I woke, my mouth tasted like filth.

I staggered into our bedroom. Lora had left the light on as a small peace offering and was asleep under the quilt, her face waxen and unhappy.

I undressed, put out the light, lay down beside her, crippled with grief and guilt, my bags all packed. The body has a mind of its own. I touched her.

Her flesh felt good to me. Her flesh has always felt good to me. I rose against her.

It seemed a form of betrayal to want her now, to want so much to leave her and yet to want to hold and stroke and be inside her.

Still in her dormancy, waking to me, she said my name. We curled into each other. The spark of our physical passion, the single light that had never gone out of our friendship, glowed in the dark. "I love you, Abner," Lora said as we began.

It felt so good, smooth and seamless as always, all the parts of us fitting perfectly and with knowledge, and we called out to each other in the dark as our bodies slithered and slammed against each other.

Yet even in that consummation I kept my distance. Even in that I held back bitter tears for the falseness of it.

For I knew the difference, even as I panted and moaned into her ear, between this thick mutuality and the airy, angelic love-making of our beginnings, when we had become one creature reaching for the stars, not two separate animals striving to get off.

So we pumped and groaned together in the darkness. And when we finished pulling at each other's flesh and were done, Lora wept. "Oh, Abner," she cried, holding me, "how did this happen to us? We used to love each other so much. We used to be so proud of ourselves as a family. Abner, what's going to happen to us?"

I felt the spear go through me again, a terror to be so ordinary and so alone.

"Abner?" pleaded my wife in a small, frightened voice. "Abner, what are we going to do?"

But I didn't know if there was any "we" left any more, and I didn't know anything to do about it.

The one thing I did know was Lora's preference for deception. "Everything will be okay," I crooned, comforting her.

"Oh, Abner, I love you so much," said my wife, sobbing against me in the soft darkness. "Oh, I wish you knew."

And that too, my wife's love and need, along with a picnic lunch packed by her as a last caring gesture, I take with me in the car on the road to New York City.

And wonder how to leave these things behind.

My stated plan is first to visit family and friends in New York. But I have a hidden agenda: To be blunt, I am going to New York to get laid.

Yes, I will begin my journey with a small act of sexual mastery in the city of my birth. This is symbolic, a gesture of separation from domestic life, a way back to myself.

As an ambition it is crass, I know, a flash in the pan. I don't care. I have been serious and responsible for years, and I am sick of it. I will find a coed young and sweet in the Museum of Modern Art or a svelte stranger at a singles bar or visit an old flame carrying a bulge in my pants to give her the idea. Someone else's mouth, someone else's breasts and hips, my body wrapped in someone else's.

I need that. I need to fuck myself clean of the past, and then go on.

The wheels of the Plymouth are gobbling up the miles. I have broken out.

A stupid fantasy. Reactive, merely, I think, gazing out the window of the rest-stop cafeteria, my hands around a styrofoam container of coffee. Though the view of the parking area changes from moment to moment as cars and people whiz in and out, it nonetheless remains absolutely the same. I could whiz in and out of a dozen women that same way.

As they lurch out of their cars, the travelers pull at the seats of their pants and dresses, unsticking themselves, and stagger inside for bad coffee at a high price. A rest stop is a lonely place, I think. After three hours of driving, I am feeling alienated.

Halfway to New York, I imagine a scenario with Amy Solomon, my old lover, that busty "girl" now in her middle thirties. For *three years* we were lovers, and with Amy, too, something had happened deeper than I could have imagined.

Yet nothing had happened, except we had come to hate each other, and I couldn't remember why, why really, except because—because—because love goes bad like an old side of beef.

Ten years ago we had parted into others' arms. I escaped to Mars in California, and she stayed in New York to do well as a graphic designer, living in her cheap railroad flat downtown while she banked money for her "future."

I knew that apartment, knew its nooks and crannies as I knew Amy's own nooks and crannies. From mutual friends, I also knew that Amy was alone again and feeling a thirty-five-year-old female despair.

And now this was the future, and I was on my way toward her, with the graphic design to hustle her into bed. Speech after long silence. I still knew which drawer she kept her diaphragm in. I could accomplish the seduction. We would not even interrupt our play while she stuck her fingers up inside to check the surgical rubber membrane crouched safely under the pelvic bone, *contra naturam*. Come in me, she moans. With the security of our latex miracle, we fuck our brains out.

Poor Amy. She so much wanted children, and now it doesn't look as if she will have them. Another womb vandalized by the Sexual Revolution.

In the sterile highway rest stop, thick shame settles over me. The styrofoam cup with the cold pool of coffee in it sits on the table like a monument to transiency. I realized that I could not do it. Too much sadness arose out of the heat and odor of our past together for me to use the entrance to that womb again. Between her legs was a place that smelled like my own failure. *Danger*, warned my inner voice: After she puts in the birth control and lays herself down, she'll have knives of desperation waiting for you. Leave her alone.

And if I found a young lovely I did not know and *shtupped* her—fine, and then? Then I would go in the bathroom and look in the mirror, and it would be the same old me—no new birth at all.

So the plan to go to New York City seemed yet another trick I had played on myself. Amy was the past, a way of escaping backwards, and if I wanted a casual stranger, I didn't need New York: Everywhere you go, lovely young women wait with membranes already lubricated.

But what, I thought, if instead I were again to be an itinerant traveler on the crust of the planet, completely on my own, all failures left behind—a kind of son of that young man who, small and distant in my mind's eye, had hitchhiked to California ten years before.

Yes, something still was operating in my nearly bankrupt poet's brain. This was better than a plan. It was a work of art: to retrace my steps, singing songs of experience as I had sung the songs of innocence before.

The symmetry alone was alluring: I would take a trip to Mars.

I dumped the styrofoam cup in the trash, I turned my car around.

I was on my own. Now no one in the world knew where I was, no one could say where I was going. I was free. I didn't need to *work it out* with anyone. It had been a long ten years.

Thank you, Cyna, for reminding me again to be the familiar cowboy herdsman of my soul.

I drove, alternating between huge crests of exhilaration and troughs of dark fear, and knew them both as appropriate responses to being on a vision quest. Tape-loops of horrors and humiliations with Lora and the kids played in my mind as I drove. I felt great pleasure to see the station wagon eating the road, for each mile of gray macadam disappearing underneath the hood was a small revenge—

A mile for every time the little bastards had refused to help me carry groceries upstairs. A mile for every broken agreement, every chore left undone because they knew that their mother would protect them from any punishment. Five miles for the paintings on the walls, ten for every double bind she put me through, for every self-serving illogic—

We are going out after dinner. Lora makes an offer: "You pick up the babysitter, I'll do the dishes."

Done. I get the babysitter, who lives out on the Lake Road.

"The phone didn't stop ringing," Lora volunteers, explaining why the dishes are not washed when I get back.

After the movie, I take the babysitter home. When I get back, the dishes are still in the sink, so I check reality with Lora:

"You're going to do the dishes, right?"

"Well," Lora begins, "I think we should talk about that." Then she suggests a new deal: She'll do the dishes, if I will do part of the shopping tomorrow.

But the shopping is, by prior deals, Lora's chore.

We fight. Lora says she doesn't understand why we fight.

Pennsylvania, Ohio . . .

Scenarios of helplessness played themselves out on my retina; radio stations faded in and out as I passed through time zones. I missed my CB; it would have been fun to listen to the language of the road while I drove. I blamed the theft on Lora, who would never lock the car door. "I was in a hurry," she would say. Or, "I was carrying packages." Or, "I expected to be going right back." The excuses made no sense—locking the door required only putting the button down before kicking the door shut, no harder than not locking it. The underlying meaning was a political statement: The Free Woman will accept no restraints. In the silverware drawer, for example, there is an "organizer," a plastic box with compartments for knives, forks, spoons. Lora throws the silverware *crosswise* to the organizer on *top* of the compartments. "I was in a hurry," she says. Or, "What difference does it make?" Or, "Don't be so uptight. You're very uptight for a poet, do you know that?"

Yes, I knew that. Drawers left open, car door unlocked, silverware scattered across the compartments, tops of jars not tightened so they slip out of the hand when picked up and splash on floor and clothing, even the refrigerator door left ajar several times a week, not by the children. Is that why I feel the chill on my bones?

I slept at rest stops on a narrow foam mattress in the back of the station wagon and woke early each morning, joints stiff, mouth furred, and started driving again.

Indiana, Illinois . . .

I subscribe to a weekly poetry newsletter—not too inspiring a periodical, but I like to look through it. Every week, Lora throws it out soon after it arrives.

I don't catch on for a while that this is a form of torture.

But who could believe such a thing? What's the point? Lora subscribes to a West Coast art weekly. If I find it where I don't want it to be, I put it on her desk. Isn't that how normal people operate?

Each time, she comes up with an almost believable excuse:

"Oh, I thought it was last week's." "I think I put it on your desk—did you look?" Finally: "Well, you shouldn't just leave it lying around, if you want me to straighten up the living room like we agreed I would."

Ten years were gone, they could never come back. They were not a total loss—I had raised children, gotten an education, written poems, learned something about love, obligation and betrayal. I knew things I had not known before.

But I might have had all that anyway. I might have found a woman who had no children and who wanted to have children with me. I might have found a woman who wanted to be reasonable. Maybe she would not have been an artist with the wild genius of Lora Sachsman. Maybe she would have wanted a life without illustrations of genitals on the living room wall—

Lora is standing in a little pool of blood that has trickled down her leg. She has gotten her period and wants to announce it to her family in a memorable manner. Sometimes she forgets to put in a Tampax, sometimes she forgets to take one out. Sometime during almost every month, Lora ends up standing in family space, bleeding onto the floor.

When I utter a reproach, she responds, "What's the big deal? Why are you so damn uptight all the time?"

Iowa, Nebraska . . .

Sometimes I drove off the Interstate and through one of those little towns whose main street had been the highway in the days before the Interstate was built and I would stop for coffee there, imagining what it would be like to stay, find a room and a job and make a life there, where no one I knew would ever find me again.

Why not? There was a library in the town, they had lectures at the local community college. I could find a job, teach college or drive a pickup, merge into the invisible life of America, yes, live among them and be one of them. Why not? Didn't they speak my native language and see the same movies? Yes, I could find out their dreams and write the poems of that place and make love to their tough country waitresses.

But of course it was a dream of oblivion, not of self-knowledge—another trick. So I would leave an extra tip, note my fantasy of the waitress in my journal and drive Main Street back onto the Interstate. I had my own road, and Cyna kept me company.

The further I drove, the dimmer the tape loops of domestic misery became. As if broadcast from Athens, New York, they drifted off like weak radio signals, warping out in the middle of a story.

Somewhere in Utah, I rented a motel room in order to shower, watch TV and sleep, expanded, in a big double bed. Early in the morning, I dreamt.

A picture postcard comes for me in the mail. The photograph is of a vaguely familiar man and a vaguely familiar woman driving separate cars. They are very happy to report their recent marriage. But the postcard has arrived late, after I had already received from somewhere else the news of their impending divorce. . . .

When I woke, it took me several moments to remember where I was. I showered again, storing it up, then dressed and went outside. A street in America. The summer air was sharp with intimations of high heat later in the day. I was thirty-five years old, half done. My knees felt stiff, the creakings of middle age already sounding in my bones.

I pointed the Plymouth west again. In the early light, my shadow stretched out ahead of me on the highway, pulling me after it to California.

CHAPTER 13

And when you get to the Pacific Ocean, turn right.

Route One, that highway through heaven, is not a serious thoroughfare. It is a toy road, the kind you draw when you're a kid, two windy lanes bisected with a dotted line. On one side, the ocean arches out from the coastline to marry the sky; on the other side rise the wooded California hillsides. Pictures from a storybook. A former northern Californian myself, I felt I was coming home.

Mars and I didn't write to each other much, but I knew the outlines: Smog and trendy women had taught him that he was a northerner after all. Instead of following the Los Angeles lights to that pot of Ding Dongs at the end of the rainbow, he had made an about-face, gone semi-organic and lived now with other people in a house in Mendocino County, among the Redwoods.

I called him from the road. A woman who introduced herself as Rose said she would give him the message that I was close.

I didn't know what I would find, and I didn't know if I would stay, but it was the right place to begin. I wasn't thinking much about the future, and that was how I knew I was on the right path.

The California cities have a relentless sense of commerce, Carmel and Big Sur are trendy and touristy, but in the counties north of San Francisco, longhairs, artists and plain folks still live by their wits in the woods. I know I am supposed, now that the world has returned to its ordinary calculations, to take a sardonic tone about the remnants of the hippies, but I still measure them with the divine yardstick of those years when it seemed the world might in fact give itself a shake and change forever. That was what I wanted again now: change forever. So I came without judgements, a seeker of my own freedom.

The town of Elk was a tiny dot on the coast route between San Francisco and the Oregon border. I almost missed both it and the restaurant at which Mars worked part-time: a log cabin set back from the road, with a sign across the front in fancy pink script: *Rosie's*. The *o* was a many-petalled rose whose stem looped up over the *s* to dot the *i* with a thorn.

Stiff with driving and breathless with anticipation, I walked in. It was small place, a counter with half a dozen stools and a few tables. Signs behind the counter advertised "Home-Made Soup" and "Home-Made Bread," and a chalkboard listed the menu for the day.

A couple of longhairs at a table in the corner looked up as I came in. A round-faced young woman engrossed in a book behind the counter didn't.

And there was Mars, wiping his hands as he came out of the kitchen. He looked a little older—the red of his beard touched with gray, something leaner in his expression than I remembered—but it was Mars, unmistakable by the way he totally embarrassed me by giving a huge war whoop when he saw me at the door, by his manly embrace, by the pounding fist of welcome on my back, by the way he pushed me to arm's length and stood hip-cocked to look me over, as if he were deciding whether to approve me for the county or not. I noted lines in the skin around his eyes as he grinned at me. And it was unmistakably me, paunchier and wearied, who tugged at his beard and grinned into his eyes and told him it was good to see him.

"Good to see you too, man," he said softly. He banged my shoulder one more time, then pulled me over to Rose, who had put her book down. "Rose," he began, putting a light brogue on for the blarney, "this is not just a frriend, this is my oldest, my dearrest, and my dumbest frriend, Abnerrr Minsky, inventor of the Follies. Be careful, lass, the boy is an extraorrrdinary seducer, he'll steal your heart and your underwear both if you aren't careful, he's a—"

"Shut up, Mars," she said, "people are trying to eat." She was about thirty, I guessed, with a round, forthright Irish face and a chipped tooth in her smile. She was wearing a sweatshirt and hadn't done anything much to make herself look pretty. She stuck out her hand, and I shook it.

"Rose," said Mars, subsiding somewhat, "is the proprietor of this establishment."

I looked around again. The place had the feel of an old-style Brooklyn luncheonette, but a lot quieter. A few handmade wooden artifacts, like the highly polished edging around the counter and the bases of the cake displayers, gave it some country class. It was nice, and I told her so.

Rose set a cup of coffee down on the counter for me.

"You want a piece of pie?" Mars offered. "Home-made. By Rose."

"Coffee's fine," I said. "Thanks."

Mars took a cup of decaf for himself, set it down on my side of the counter and just grinned at my profile for a while.

"Mars hasn't talked about anything else since I told him you called," Rose said. "I never saw him so excited."

"It ain't every day world-class events happen, Rosie," he told her. "You got to recognize them when they do."

She looked at him placidly for a moment, then said, "You want the afternoon off?"

"Let's get out of here," Mars said to me, sliding off his stool. "Thank you, Rose."

Rose picked up her book again. This time I could see it was Blake. Blake among the Redwoods—I liked it. "'He who desires but acts not breeds pestilence,'" I quoted at her.

"I know," said Rose.

"What are you, on vacation?"

"Lora and I are probably splitting up."

Mars's mouth opened and closed. "What happened?"

"The Vietnam War. I think I was only staying in it because I had already invested so much." I was behind the wheel, driving county roads at Mars's direction. "But I finally figured out that just because something is sad and horrible doesn't necessarily mean it's good for you." I had pages of illustrations for him to look at.

"So what are you gonna do?" he asked when I was done.

"I have to be back in Athens at the beginning of September. But the summer is mine—want to go to India?" He laughed. "I don't know exactly. I have to figure out a plan. I'm thirty-five years old—if I'm going to have a life, I better start soon."

"Yeah, soon," said Mars, in a tone that suggested he was thinking of something private. There was a moment of quiet. "There's the house," he said, pointing out the window.

It was an old frame house on a bluff overlooking the ocean. Gaunt and weatherbeaten, half hidden behind trees, it seemed very isolated, half-wild, like the setting for a gothic novel. Mars was living in it with Rose and her old man Peter.

Highway One passed in front of the hillside, but you had to go off onto a county road to get to the house. We drove up the hill and came up into the driveway around the rear. Close up, the structure looked in bad shape, the paint flaking off the salt-cracked siding, windows broken upstairs, the grounds unkempt. A radical fixer-upper. I followed Mars in.

Inside, the house was impressive. The rooms were huge, high-ceilinged and dark, with wooden floors, doors and window sashes, and the walls were papered with intricate flowery prints. The stairway was wide and wooden, with five large bedrooms upstairs. Everything was sparsely furnished, empty-looking, as if people were just moving in or out.

Peter, Mars explained, was being bankrolled by an old friend of Rose's in San Rafael to buy and remodel houses along this section of the coast. The money-man (his name was Barry, but Mars called him Big Bucks) had bought up properties before the boom and was now dealing them slowly back onto the market at big profits.

From the windows in the wooden cathedral of the dining room, I could make out the ocean through the screen of trees. Mars set out thick grainy bread and jars of Rose's home-made jam, and we smoked a joint for old time's sake.

By 7 o'clock, when Rose came home, the summer sun was angled down in the sky and the house, shaded under trees and loose with age, began to get chilly. Rose had brought with her half a pie that might not make it through the next day at the restaurant. Chopping and sautéing together, we concocted a casserole while baby potatoes roasted in the oven. We ate.

Peter came in past dusk. We were hunched into sweaters against the chill, but he was dressed in a teeshirt that showed his biceps. He was good-looking, with regular features, a deep tan and black hair pulled back into a pony-tail. Tall, dark and handsome.

"Hi, babe," he said to Rose and gave her a hug. "Mars," he added with a nod, like a whole sentence of greeting.

"Peter," Mars said back. "Peter, this is Abner."

I rose and stuck out my hand.

"Abner," he said, another complete sentence. "We've been expecting you." He didn't smile, gave my hand a brief shake, then turned away. "Any dinner left, hon?"

Rose had put aside casserole and pie for him, and there were still potatoes left in the bowl. She brought the food out of the warming oven and set it down on the table.

"You gonna stay?" he asked me, spooning casserole onto his plate.

He was either rude or into obscure poetry. “I don’t know,” I said. “You inviting me?”

“Depends,” he said. “You want to work?”

“Peter,” Rose reminded him, “guests?”

“Guests,” he said without embarrassment. “He asked,” he told Rose and gave her a little smile I couldn’t read. “Barry wants to get the house ready,” he said.

“No,” Rose told him immediately. “No. I don’t like—I don’t want to have to move again.”

Peter looked at her. “Can I have the potatoes?”

“I mean it,” she said. “I don’t want to move again. Why can’t we stay here and you fix up some other house for Barry?”

“We’ve got a year,” Peter said flatly, imparting information. “Pass the potatoes?”

“Yeah, a year of you tearing the walls down around us. I don’t want it, Peter,” she said again.

“It’s not for a while, Rosie,” he said.

“Thanks for your sympathy.” She pressed her lips together, and he smiled, as if he appreciated sarcasm. She made an exasperated face at him and finally passed the bowl of roasted potatoes.

He served himself and began to eat.

I was tired and went to bed early on a foam mattress in one of the empty bedrooms upstairs. I lay looking out the window into the abstract darkness.

Would I get divorced and have to see my failure in the faces of the people I knew? I imagined Hannah with a mother and stepfather and a father and stepmother, cashiered between broken homes like Eli and Ella, herself broken a little inside—wounded in her ontology, as Lora sometimes said of Ella.

Outside, a million crickets sang to the stars. Inside, as I drifted toward sleep, my parents began to remonstrate with me. How well I knew those voices! *Don’t Eli and Ella deserve something from you? To have this happen to them twice!—after you’ve been their father?*

But what’s the problem? my old man asked from the grave. He wanted a clear answer, something to weigh, like a half pound of lox. What’s eating you up?

Nothing, I tell him. I’m just miserably unhappy all the time. I made a bad bargain—does that mean I gave up my right forever to a little human comfort?

Oh, what a loud and silent shrug comes over the galactic

telephone line, what a cosmic raising of the eyebrows. No, as a matter of fact, they don't believe that people have a right to anything, let alone happiness. *Maybe if you made the bargain, you have to stick to it, one of them says, and the other nods forever in agreement.*

All of a sudden I am wide awake with anger. How easily I can make myself feel like a child gone astray. *You are thirty-five years old,* I instruct myself. *It is a little late for you to be worrying about disappointing your parents. Why the sudden failure of nerve, Minsky? Divorce is unpleasant, but a lot of people go through the pain and make a new bargain with their old spouse. Do you think the solution is worse than the problem?*

I imagined myself divorced and in the market again, looking over the eligible women, wondering what combination of mistakes and failures brought them to their thirties without a real life of their own. . . . I play the singles scene, have "adult" relationships, a modern life, get my daughter for holidays and summers. Strange flesh, intricate crevices of someone else's life, work of getting to know all the earthy details of bedroom and kitchen—to go through that again! Hannah, this is Lisa; Hannah, this is Penny; Hannah, this is Sharon; Hannah, this is—

Or to be a single parent—because I could never, never leave Hannah to her, for her to confound, to fashion into a clone of herself. A single father, not knowing how, alone as winter evenings close in with no one to talk it over with or hand it over to or share—.

But what is the alternative? To stay together for the sake of the children? That final blurring of cowardice with obligation?

I felt sick at heart with homelessness to be again at the beginning of something I could not yet recognize, starting over in Mars's house in California.

At last, long after the crickets had grown quiet, the internal voices blurred and I fell asleep.

CHAPTER 14

Morning in the country. My dark night of the soul seemed distant in the sunlight pouring through the window, and I rose with energy. Downstairs, a note from Mars told me he had a hauling job, make myself at home. Rose and Peter were both gone. I wandered outside.

The wooded grounds around the house were, like the house itself, untended, run down and punctuated with parts of things—half a wooden chair, a rotted ladder, a caved-in metal bucket, a rusted rake. The wide front porch was rickety, with floorboards warped and rotting off their nails.

Behind the house, away from the ocean, was a long rectangular fenced yard with two weatherbeaten sheds at the far end. In one quadrant of the yard, the ghostly outline of another year's garden still remained—dead brushy vines hanging off wooden stakes, long scraps of black plastic on the ground, everything overgrown with weeds.

The gate resisted, then gave way, and I walked in. A huge tree stump took the center of the yard, defining everything around it. Its top, thick and weathered to grayness, formed a round platform four feet across. The garden was narrowed because of it and the natural path from the gate to the sheds detoured around it. It was the central object here. Its thick roots disappeared into the ground, overgrown with tall weeds.

What a tree it must have been. What a hole it must have made high in the air. How the mighty had fallen. Feeling unaccountably stirred, I climbed onto the stump that remained, dominating it, to survey the weatherbeaten sheds and the sunlit, shrubby woods beyond. In me too there was something deep and well-attached and dead that shaped all the rest. In my inner garden too there was a great tree reduced to an impotent stump blocking and determining all other growth.

When I turned again toward the house, Peter was lounging against the doorjamb, watching me.

He pushed himself erect and came toward me then, slightly pigeon-toed, with a rolling, bouncy gait. He was wearing jeans, a fresh tee shirt and a beat-up cowboy hat, its brim curled up around the sides. He was a physical guy, thick-thighed and solid-looking, not fat but bulky—something for Rose to hold on to, I thought.

He pushed through the gate into the yard, and I jumped down off the stump.

When he reached me, he stuck out his hand, as if we were meeting for the first time. His mouth played with a cocky smile that must, I thought, have gotten him in trouble other times in his life. He was wanting to start over, I guess, for as we shook hands, he said, "I'm sorry about last night—I gave you a hard time."

I shrugged. "I thought that was just your personality."

The smile widened lazily. "It is. That's what I'm apologizing for."

I didn't exactly forgive him, but I accepted the apology.

"They used to keep chickens and a goat here," he was saying, pointing toward the sheds. "Rose wants to get a garden going, but she's busy. And Mars isn't a gardener." He sat down on the tree stump. "Mars said you're on the road for a while."

"In a way."

"What I meant last night was—there's a project here that needs to get done. Maybe you can help do it."

"I'm no gardener either."

"I need someone to help clean out the sheds, clean up the yard. It's grunt work. Rose would help on a garden."

"It's not exactly my line of work."

He paused to look me over, and I saw myself through his eyes: shirt *and* undershirt, cords, foam-soled sports shoes. An overweight city fellow standing next to a tree stump. He shrugged. "Mars thought you might want to."

Well, in fact, I could imagine it: laboring hard in the sun, with time to write and wander in the Redwoods. Why not? I didn't much like Peter, but I didn't have to.

He kicked the stump. "I want to start by dynamiting this sucker."

Dynamiting it? The stump is mine, I thought in alarm. "I would want to dig it up," I said.

"Dig it up?" He looked appalled. "That'd take weeks."

But for once I knew what I wanted. I had made the vital metaphor, and even if was just superstition, I was going to believe it: The stump was the lump in my heart, and if I was going to stay, I had to uproot it. I spread my palms out to Peter. "I'm willing to do the job, but that's my wage: I get to dig up the stump."

He looked at me speculatively, thinking it over. Maybe he was considering if I was crazy. Then he shrugged and put his foot on the stump again. "Okay," he said. "Fine. It's all yours."

I had jeans, though they seemed ostentatiously new in comparison with Peter's faded denims. I had to borrow a pair of cracked and dirty workboots from him, a symbolism neither of us acknowledged as I pulled them on. I felt like a greenhorn—another immigrant Minsky.

When I was dressed for the job, Peter got a shovel out of the little toolshed beside the house and, balancing it easily over his shoulder, preceded me back into the yard and stabbed it into the ground. He gazed back up at the house. "How are you on roofs?" he wanted to know.

"I'll hold the ladder," I told him.

After he climbed up to look around, I tore weeds away around the stump and started hacking at the baked earth with the shovel.

"If you wet the ground first," Peter called, supervising from above, "it makes the digging easier." His tone of voice mildly suggested my stupidity for not having thought of it myself.

I dragged the hose out and let the ground soak, then jabbed the shovel into the wet ground and threw dirt off to the side. Bending and straightening, I had managed a small hole when Peter came down the ladder. I was sweating hard.

"Let me show you something." He grabbed the shovel, pointed its tip into the earth, stepped on it hard and peeled off a clump of sod about three inches thick and as deep as the shovel would go; he dropped it over his left shoulder. "See?" He peeled off another full shovel's worth. "You don't really have to work so hard." He did another, flipped the dirt off to his left again. "Get into a rhythm and it moves right along."

I labored under his direct supervision for half a dozen strokes. "That's better," he said at last and went back up the ladder, leaving me both grateful and bruised-in-the-ego.

After a while, my palms began to blister. "Gloves," he said when I complained, "I forgot." He examined the little red circles with his fingertips. "Been awhile since you worked, huh? Hold on." He fetched from the house a pair of work gloves and a tube from which he smeared brown ointment on my hands. The combination of casual contempt and paternal kindness kept me silent, jerked in two directions. I pulled the gloves on, stripped down to my tee shirt and, feeling fat, went back to digging.

By the time Mars came back, Peter had gone and I was sitting, dirty, sweaty and exhausted, on the stump, looking down into the small pit I had created in front of it.

"You're a strange one, Abner Minsky," Mars said when I explained about the stump. "But, hey, I'm glad you'll be sticking around a while."

"A garden?" Rose beamed that night at dinner. "I wouldn't lift a finger to get this place ready to sell—but a garden!"

"You could have put in a garden anytime you wanted," Peter told her.

"Who has time?" she said, and laughed.

The next day, she came home at midmorning, changed into grungy work clothes and, first with a scythe, then with a hoe, then with her hands, started to clear the weeds. "We have to get cracking," she called to me.

She was serious about gardening, using the word "crops," as if the back yard were a farm. "We'll put in a crop of corn, a crop of tomatoes, some greenpeas, some squash." She pointed to sections of the yard as if food already grew there. "Do you like melons? And root crops—carrots, onions, potatoes. You might get to eat the corn, if you stay. But maybe not the tomatoes."

I stopped digging. "Why not the tomatoes?"

"Tomatoes ripen late. Don't you have to go back to your wife and your life?"

Ah, the wife life.

Rose cast a shrewd look into my silence. "You have a picture of her?"

I found in my wallet a photo of the four of us in Athens holding Carvel cones aloft like torches and grinning at the camera, and a separate photo of Hannah. All of a sudden, while I dug up the stump of my life, my life had dropped in for a visit.

"You look like a family, all right," Rose said. She looked deeply at the two pictures. "Why'd you run away?"

"I couldn't figure out how many kids to list on my resumé."

She squinted over at me. "You got a nice family," she said. "You're lucky." She gave me back the pictures and got back to work.

Watery blisters bubbled on my hands. Muscles I didn't know I possessed had mouths that bit me, and I woke up stiffer each morning than I had been the night before. The muscles in my fingers could not be relied on to follow simple commands for buttoning and tying. The long muscles in my thighs froze. I pulled my socks and pants on like an exhibit in a Jerry Lewis telethon.

But after a few days, the blisters burst; a few days more and they calloused over. The stiffness got worse and then began to subside.

"Let's look at the sheds," Peter said, interrupting my digging. "The stump isn't the only thing."

The stump isn't the—. It was the end of the third week of my sojourn. I had dug a cold frame for broccoli and lettuce; I had taken turns with Rose rototilling the garden area, letting the machine pull me back and forth like a horse. I had helped Rose plant seed corn and tomato starts. I had scythed the weeds to ground level from the fence to the shed walls. No, the stump wasn't the only thing.

But it was, for some reason, Peter's preference to act that way. I let it go, playing Hired Hand to his Disgruntled Boss, and followed him into the larger of the two sheds. It was a stuffy landscape of broken cages, strips of chicken wire, slats from wooden boxes. The surfaces were thick with gummy dust and the place still smelled feathery and close, though it had been years since chickens lived there. "Not much to take out of here," Peter said.

The other shed was a crowded closet, so filled with metal bedsprings, rusted garden tools, doodads and parts of things that we couldn't walk through to the back wall. "Let's do it," he said.

He backed his pickup to the fence and we lugged. The job was clear and simple, and we worked without talking, piling the bed of the pickup with junk. It was midday, and the sun beat down on us.

After the truck was loaded, I stood sweating while Peter brought two bottles of Coors out of the house. He popped the caps on an edge of the truck, handed one over and slid onto the ground in the shade of the cab. I settled next to him.

We nursed the beers in silence. But when you work with a man, sunshine and sweat are a lubricant. I asked him some questions and he told me his answers. Most of it I already knew from Mars. He was a Midwesterner, from a town outside Decatur, Illinois. His father, a contractor, had been a crabbed, fierce man, protective of what belonged to him—wife, kids, house, business—and not much concerned with what didn't. The old man had taught Peter tools—taught him and forced him till he was good at carpentry, construction, plumbing, electrical work, till Peter had fled to California just to escape him. In California, he found Rose and when Rose's old friend Barry—Big Bucks—agreed to bankroll her ambition to own a restaurant, he had a way to fit Peter into his plans too. So here he was. It was a simple story: He had become his father.

No doubt he didn't see it that way.

I told him the outlines of me and Lora.

"I was married once—Mars tell you that?" Mars hadn't. "Jewish girl, in fact. I was twenty, I knew her a few weeks. After we got married, she told me she still wanted to sleep with other guys—she said it was a way to make the world better, nobody be possessive any more. I said, What's wrong with being possessive?—you're mine or you're not." He took a long hit of beer. "She picked the wrong guy. Dump her," he advised me bluntly. "If someone is bleeding you, pull them off. You got to protect yourself."

He didn't know me well enough to offer advice, but he didn't seem to know that. Meanwhile, the subject had made him loquacious.

"I care about Rose a lot," he went on, "but I'm not sentimental about her—I learned that from my ex-wife. I was sentimental about *her*, I thought I needed her. That's slavery, man. Now I don't need anybody and I don't owe anybody. Rose'll do whatever's best for her, and I'll do what's best for me. That's what everybody does, except they dress it up in philosophy."

He squinted over at me. "Like you and me," he said. "You're doing work I'd have to pay somebody to do. I'm exploiting you. But you want to do it, so we both get what we want. If you don't, you split."

"I guess so," I said. He was dressing something up in philosophy too. I didn't know exactly what, but I knew he wasn't offering friendship. He was talking walls, not bridges, as if he wanted me to know not to depend on him.

"We gotta get this shit to the dump," he decided abruptly. He finished his beer, tossed the bottle into the bed of the pickup as he rose, pulled the door open and, all business again, climbed behind the wheel. I went around the other way and mounted into the cab, and we drove to the dump to get rid of the garbage.

The digging was a meditation. As I wielded the shovel in rhythm under the hot sun, images passed before my eyes, occasional music for poems would sound in my ear, and I would come back to myself surprised to be in a fenced yard above the ocean.

Addressing the stump as the blocked life I had made for myself, I dug down, first with the unsubtle shovel and then with hand tools, following every thick wooden root into its smaller tributaries down to its delicate tendrilly end, pulling it up with worms and dirt.

As the weeks passed, I saw that my arms had filled out. When, in the privacy of my room, I "made a muscle," a handsome muscle actually popped up. My skin was brown now, sun-darkened into long gloves that ended where my tee shirt sleeves began, there was a collar of darkness on my neck, and my forehead was burnished by sunshine. I was looking pretty good for a fat man, I thought. I felt strong.

Yes, I told myself, I had found something more effective than fucking myself clean of the past. I was working myself clean, sweating out old hurts in the sun, beating them to death with shovel and trowel.

My paunch had shrunk. I wasn't skinny, but the bag of fat had disappeared and left a membrane of muscle underneath. My reflection in the mirror was not divided in two; what lay below my waist was no longer a separate hemisphere, out of sight. Even my cock, that buried god, looked bigger and more alert.

Peter was right. He was exploiting me, and there was something in it for me. Was that Cyna's voice I heard welcoming me back?

CHAPTER 15

Yes, there are buried gods. I had neglected Cyna, my genius and friend, and she, with no man in whose mouth she could sing, had gone to sleep.

Awakened now, she did not recriminate but resumed her place: someone to talk with, someone to show the pictures to, someone who understood several levels at once—Cyna the knowing, Cyna the sardonic, Cyna the beautiful, Cyna the reverent, Cyna the thoughtful, Cyna pal-of-mine—my teacher Cyna who weightless came along and did not bite my ankles or complain but said: Go slow, go deep, and write it down, man.

In short, friends of poetry, I remembered how to practice my profession.

It was a familiar routine: half a day of working hard, half a day of wandering and writing, a reprise of my life the first time I had come to California so long ago. In the morning, I labored. In the afternoon, I took my notebook to the cliffs across the highway and stared back at the huge arched eyeball of the Pacific, feeling like Robinson Jeffers; or I stayed in the empty house, peering out the upstairs windows like Emily Dickinson; or I roamed the tame woods of the neigborhood like Robert Frost at home in New England. In the evening, I prepared food with and for Mars, Peter and Rose. Cyna was there for all of it, I felt her moving inside me, idiosyncratic and full of thrust. I remembered Lora, but I did not miss her.

Rose kept a journal in which, she admitted shyly, she wrote poems. "You ever get them published?" I asked while we weeded the cabbages.

"I don't send them out."

"How come?"

She shrugged. "They're no good, really."

Minsky's rule: When people say their poems are no good, never ask to see them anyway. "Can I see some?" Minsky asked, playing cannon fodder.

She swabbed sweat off her face, wiped her hands on her jeans and preceded me into the house.

"I'll show you just a few," she decided. I dropped into a

kitchen chair while she went upstairs and came back clutching a folder with pages falling out of it. Her round face was more nervous than I had seen it. "If you hate them, say so, okay?"

"Sure," I agreed. She chose half a dozen, typed on the ancient manual typewriter in her room, with revisions lightly marked on them in pencil.

I took a deep breath.

The first one, a little rhymed portrait of someone eating, had wit and charm (that was a relief) and the last lines contained an elegant judgement on him:

Imprisoned in the personal
Like honey in a glass of tea.

The other five poems were also about food or eating—the natural poesy of a restauranteur. They were all short, colloquial, understated and without falseness.

"You *really* like them?" she wanted to know, her round face flashing out beams of pleasure. "Really?"

It is so easy to make us poets happy.

"Running a restaurant is a great thing for a poet," she told me, no longer nervous. "It's like being a bartender." We were snacking on yogurt and brown bread with honey. "Some days I think I can tell everything about people by the way they eat."

"What do you know about me?" I asked, halting my second slice of bread on its way in.

She threw me a shrewd look and then laughed. "I already started writing a poem about you," she said. "You keep eating when you aren't hungry any more, Abner."

"You should open an office in the restaurant," I told her. I put the slice of bread aside, and we went back to work.

Rose Delaney presents: Sweetpeas. They went in salads and casseroles, only a few at first, then a cornucopia. Then weirdly shaped organic carrots too small to pluck but sweet enough to eat. Coming soon: more zucchini than we could ever use—zucchini soup and fried zucchini at our table and at Rosie's Restaurant. July passed, August began. The young corn was just beginning to tassle, the tomatoes were green marbles full of promise. The garden, as even Peter acknowledged, was a great success.

When I had enough of the stump exposed, I took steel

wedges and a mallet to it, cracking off pieces down to the root and sawing off the hanging blocks of wood. Then I went on digging.

Still attached to the surrounding earth by its network of roots, the stump hung over its dark hole as if defiant of gravity. I left it that way for days, in proof of my incipient triumph, while I did other things, and then Peter wrapped the stump in chains, hooked them to the winch on his pickup and started the motor. There was a metallic rattling as the chains tightened into a wrestler's hug around the thick torso of the stump. The stump resisted, battling back against the truck, hanging in there groaning while metal machine whines sliced the air. And then, with a thick sucking noise and a final dull plop, it tore away from its rooted place and fell on its side, a gnarly and tentacled beast lying dead in the dirt.

Mars and Rose hurrahed. "Now what're you gonna do with it?" Peter asked, killing the engine, his voice slightly mocking about my love affair with the stump.

"After you slaughter the beast, you cut it up for food," I told him, feeling pure satisfaction flow into the hole of my poor damaged heart.

"Here lies one of Minsky's greatest works," intoned Mars, clapping me on the shoulder while I grinned like crazy. Peter climbed into the pickup and dragged the stump into the woodshed. The next day he tutored me sternly in the use of mallet and ax.

By the sweat of my brow, this stump would heat the house this winter.

And after that there would be nothing left of it but memory. Except that during these weeks, the stump's thick, muscular roots had mysteriously become my body. Like those cannibals who eat their enemies' testicles in order to acquire their potency, I seemed to have taken on the stump's sinewy strength.

And though the house would be sold and I and my work forgotten, the garden here would be forever, because of me, untrammeled and six feet wider than before—as much wider as I was tall.

The lengthened shadow of a man is history, said Emerson. I had left my mark.

By mid-August, when the summer sun reached its fiercest and the first few ears of yellow corn came to the table, I had learned enough about Peter to like him less. Every once in a while, he would smile by surprise or make a deadpan joke, and when he wanted to, he could be friendly and even charming. But his good moods were unreliable; usually he stayed silent, watchful and intimidatingly certain of himself.

Worse, he was a nag. He corrected how I did things or found fault mutely by turning his dark eyes on me till I remembered what I was or wasn't doing. Mars thought he was someone trapped and struggling with his own insecurities and character flaws. But that didn't make me enjoy being Vampire's Victim. And in the end, he simply wanted what he wanted; that was the bottom line. Sometimes he wanted to be friendly. Big deal.

"Oh, he's the boogey man all right," Mars agreed. "First time I met him I was moving a big armoire for him down a narrow stairway. I'm the professional mover, right? He gave me his tough-sheriff look and told me I was doing it all wrong." He shrugged. "It's a personality disorder." He turned a hand up. "But he was right about the cabinet."

But he was wrong the morning I was sitting in front of the empty fireplace in the living room balancing notebooks on my knees, redacting from *ur*-drafts a final working draft of a long poem. Peter came into the room and looked at me. Hi, I said. He nodded, went in the kitchen, reappeared with a cup of coffee in his hand and stood across the room scrutinizing me until I asked, "What's up?"

He turned a hand over. "There's still a lot to be done," he said.

A notebook fell as I sat up straighter. "You're saying I should be out working instead of inside writing?"

"I'm saying there's a lot that needs to get done," he repeated evenly. "Now that the stump's out," he added with tone. We looked at each other for a while, then he took a drink of coffee, nodded politely again and left.

All concentration destroyed, I sat there chewing it over. Was he my boss? The night before, he had complained that the rudimentary watering system in the garden required too much hose-dragging. "I think you could find," he had told me expressionlessly while we cleaned up from dinner, "some time to dig a few trenches."

"Yowsuh," I had told him back, "Ah jes' heah to take yo' ohders, suh."

He had not been amused.

Now here we were again. Today was, to be fair, the third day in a row that I had stopped working halfway through the morning in order to befriend my notebook. But that, Cyna assured me, was what I was in the world for, after all. Peter had each day let me know he wanted all the grass cut and the long back fence repaired. I doubted that it was my job.

"Am I here to finish the yard to his specifications by the end of the summer?" I had asked Mars, checking reality. "Did I ever agree to that?"

"You're here to visit me and have a good time," said Mars.

Working on my poem, I didn't go back out to the yard for the rest of the day. That evening, Peter had nothing to say to me.

Yes, it was time to move on. The stump was out—maybe I was ready to face my life again. And I would have left right then—I should have left right then, with the corn ripened and the tomatoes turning pink—but I had started on another project with Rose.

Rose was a kind of folk poet. More pure than I, but more poor than I, she had no home in any literary landscape. She had never even given a reading, though, and that seemed ridiculous. Mendocino County might be the country, but it wasn't Bumpkinville: The woods were filled with poets and artists, crafts were half the local industry and the county (like many provincial places), prided itself on being a "center of culture."

"For the sake of your friends," I cajoled.

"I'm scared," she said, not needing much of a push. "Will you do it with me?"

So I had agreed. While Peter and I settled into grim civility with each other, Rose and I worked at getting her poems in shape, putting notices on bulletin boards, practicing reading to each other, arranging to borrow folding chairs. The reading would happen in the nearly bare living room of the house, and restauranteur Rose insisted on providing refreshments.

Named for the city's patron saint, Rose had been raised in Santa Rosa and routed through the Catholic school system, where she had trouble with the doctrine. Sister Teresa insisted that every sin made a dark indelible blot on a person's white soul, the soul being an object something like an internal garment the size of her body which had been given to her by Jesus.

"Do you want," Sister Teresa inquired of the girls, "to cause your pure white garment from Jesus to be stained?"

Rose didn't accept this theology, and her informal survey of her seventh grade class indicated that only four girls out of thirty-three did. And even those four rolled up the waistbands of their plaid parochial-school skirts as soon as school was out, so they could show their knees. The Authorities, learning of Rose's independent sociology project, rewarded her with a forced apology to Sister Teresa, confession, penances and suspension from school for three days.

Rose told me all this in the kitchen while separating, with small, graceful Catholic-school-girl turns of the wrist, the whites of eggs from the yolks. She was making pound cake. "I was twelve years old and my mother told me I was going to Hell," she said. "So, just for spite, I started to stain my immortal soul in earnest, just like everyone else was doing. And now look at me," she beamed, a happy sinner.

They didn't go together, I thought. A dour hunk like Peter you would expect to have a hunkette of some sort, somebody tight-featured, sharp-tongued, blonde and not too bright. But Rose was neither tough, attractive, glamorous nor narrow: she was an unpretentious Irish peasant type with a round face, a gap between her front teeth and a good brain. I didn't understand how her generous smile fit his coldness.

Not that there was any need for me to understand. I was free to like her and not like him. At the end of the week was our reading; a few days later I figured to be gone. Going home, and whether I had a home to go to, was worry enough for me.

Two nights before the reading, I lay in bed and listened to Rose and Peter arguing. Many nights, alone in my room, I had tracked them in theirs, hearing the inarticulate drone of their talking, the muted rhythms of their lovemaking. Like an eavesdropper too far away to make out words or learn anything useful, I nevertheless felt excited by my familiarity with their private presence in the next chamber.

But tonight they were fighting, and loudly enough for me to make out not only the vociferous tones of her voice and his responding growl but some of the content as well.

I sat up in bed and leaned into the wall to listen.

Fragments of sentences—something to do to do with Big Bucks and the sale of the house.

"—been willing to live in places that aren't my home and

move every year and you—"

He said something.

"—not fair of you, Peter. It's not—"

His turn again, but I could not decipher it.

"—you would be here. This is about *me*—how can you not be here? I deserve—"

He was going to miss the reading. I felt oddly exhilarated by the news and, like a child overhearing his parents argue, excited by their anger, especially because I understood that they were, in a way, arguing over me. I, the impresario of Rose's poetry reading, was the cause of this trouble.

He spoke a few syllables.

"—could if you wanted to. But you don't care, Peter. You don't care about anything that—"

"Rosie—" He said her name sharply, but she overrode him.

"Tell Barry you have something else to do. Tell him you have something planned with me." She was yelling. "You think he's gonna tell you 'Screw Rose'? You think he's gonna—"

Peter said something, not raising his voice. I could imagine him being deadly rational with her, a character out of Ayn Rand.

There was a long while when I could not make out any words, and then I thought I heard her crying. Then the door opened and closed, and I heard him stamp past my door and down the stairs.

I lay awake, alone in my room next to Rosie in hers. And then, unbidden, the remembrance floated into my mind of the weeks last summer at Athens College when I had intruded even more unnoticed into a woman's life. . . .

At the Dean's request, I had filled in for three weeks as an administrator. The administrator on leave, Ms. Adrienne Siegel, had been in the job several years and her office was well lived in. I had never met her, but from a close investigation of the photographs on her bulletin board (family scenes and goofy shots of fun-with-friends), I had figured out that she was the slender, dark woman with a perm and a wide grin, and I identified, with the help of a basket of her correspondence, her parents, sister and lover. From the telephone answering machine on her desk, I even learned her voice.

The scent and sense of her rose out of her desk drawers: lip gloss and eye liner, a few sticks of sandalwood incense, homeopathic vitamins, three regular Tampax, a perfumed candle, two boxes of herbal tea. In one drawer I discovered a Charles Addams cartoon, titled "Beppo tries to save his marriage," that I too had clipped from the *New Yorker* during days of misery with Lora: A clown, in full regalia, is sitting in a wing chair across from a dowdy, dull woman. The thought balloon above his head reads, "God, she's boring. How long can I keep this smile on my face?"

It was not a funny cartoon. Finding it, I knew that Adrienne Siegel too understood something about the fleshy terror of loving, living with and hating someone.

She looked young in her photos, but over-enthusiastic birthday invitations in the correspondence basket announced her thirty-eighth. The basket also contained a current receipt from the Athens Buddhist Meditation Center. A woman of my class and race, unmarried and reaching the end of her child-bearing years, this Adrienne was a searcher and a lonely person. I felt close to her, and the sense of her female presence aroused me as I rummaged among her things. For those weeks, I had a clandestine feeling of opening up her secret places and possessing her.

The Friday before she was due back at work, she came in person to pick up her messages. She was fleshier than the photos made her seem, and her face was already lightly lining with age. Forgetting that I had never met her (I thought we were intimates), I was surprised that she acted coldly businesslike with me. Or did she know that I had violated her drawers and enjoyed her behind her closed office door? . . .

Peeper, poet and poker into lives not my own wherever I went, I finally fell asleep, one wall away from Rose.

I woke early. Rose, sitting at the kitchen table when I got there, looked ragged and underslept, her hair not brushed out. A mug of tea was getting cold in front of her. I turned on the flame under the kettle. "You don't look like you woke up yet, Rose," I told her. "Everything okay?"

She waited a long time. I sat down across from her and watched the sadness on her face. I thought I knew what was wrong, but she said, "I have a retarded sister, did I ever tell you that? They sent her away to an institution after I was born."

"No, you didn't tell me about that." The water boiled, and I made instant coffee for myself and fresh tea for Rose. "Thank you," she said. She wrapped her hands around the cup.

"You're welcome." I waited for her.

"My parents didn't like to talk about her," she said at last. "It was a kind of failure to them. They made believe she didn't exist." She shook her head wearily. "I have a sister who is defective and she got banished because of it. I don't think about it a lot, but I know that all my life, somewhere inside me, I've wondered, Was it somehow my fault? Would they do it to me?" She gave me a crooked smile. "It made me very insecure." Then she said, "Peter doesn't want to have kids."

I nodded, not knowing where we were going. "And you do?"

"*Yes I want kids*." She sounded indignant that I could have doubted it. "I'm thirty-two years old, I have to be thinking about it. He just says no, he doesn't want to. Flat out. And I'm with him, and I love him."

She wanted kids, he didn't; it was the opposite of me and Lora. Rose had blundered into a different trap. "So what are you going to do?"

"I don't know. Try to convince him, I guess. He's not coming to the reading," she said.

She told me what I knew: Peter would be gone all weekend to a meeting in Marin County with Barry and potential buyers. She tried to make it sound reasonable.

She failed. "You sound mad," I said.

She waited a long time, as if deciding something. "Peter takes good care of me. He'll do anything for me. Except—except go out of his way."

She heaved a sigh, and we sat together, both thinking about Peter. Rose loved him and served him. She had just confided in me what kept her loyal to him, if I could figure it out. She was attached to Peter, willing to serve him and accept his coldness, because he gave her a place—was that it? She was with him, not abandoned, but she had to obey. Was it a Catholic school formula?

But that was too simple, because the place she had with Peter was filled for her also with the terrifying knowledge that he might at any time disappear, abandon her—leave her defective and needy and alone. Somehow she had sought out, not only her pleasure and security, but also what made her grieve and be afraid. She had found both in Peter, and that was why she was with him.

And if I saw so easily that this was true of her, it was likely to be true of me too. Though I couldn't see it clearly, Lora was what I loved and the lure of what destroyed me, both at the same time.

Rose and I drank our morning drinks in silence: There was nothing to say. And if I felt sorry for her, and for myself too, I also felt a stab of hateful envy for Peter, for his easy ability to manage things for his benefit and fully to follow, without guilt, his own agenda.

I hadn't taken that liberty in ten years or more.

CHAPTER 16

Rose, wearing a floor-length skirt of royal blue and a white Victorian blouse with a high collar and a lacey patterned bodice, stood at the front of the living room, behind a lectern we had borrowed, and gazed out over the crowd of her friends and neighbors. She looked pale with dread, as befits a Victorian poet.

Her audience, dressed in informal country finery, sat on folding chairs that Mars and I had set up in rows: the longhairs who ate breakfast at Rosie's wearing cowboy hats and bandannas, the skinny mechanic from the Independent wearing an unlikely tie under his big Adam's apple, storekeepers and their wives dressed for town, junior faculty and spouses from the community college, a few peasant-skirted women of the local crafts collective whose work Rose sometimes put on display, local truck farmers she bought produce from spiffed up in clean jeans and shirts, two lesbian artists holding hands between their chairs, the mustachioed reporter from the local weekly (a write-up in the paper?). The room was filled.

I had gone first. Mars had given me a warm and corny introduction, and I started off with a brief poem called "Gauguin," one of the first I had ever written. It still seemed emblematic to me of my own odd poet's path, and I liked to begin readings with it, as if to keep it emblazoned on the prow of my flagship. This was the poem.

To know
what to paint
he had to get
drunk—
to paint
he had to
go away
to an island
& get drunk
all the time—
he left his job—
he went
far away

to an island
in the south
sea/

I left a beat after the ambiguous last word, read a few other poems and then got out of the way. I liked the sound of my voice, the sense of making some small change in the sensibilities behind those upturned human faces—I liked being the center of attention, too—but this was Rose's event.

Dressed in her royal colors, Rose looked beautiful as she stood at the front of the room. She licked her lips.

"Thank you for coming," she began. "Most of you people know me as a cook. Well, poetry is a kind of food, too, so I'd like to begin with a few snacks." She opened her folder and read, one after another, the little restaurant poems, her voice becoming steadily more confident. Once they caught on, the cowboys in the back whooped and dug their elbows in each other's ribs, recognizing themselves, and from everyone else she won appreciative laughter and applause. The pallor on her cheeks changed gradually to blush.

After the restaurant poems, she read several "poetic" meditations on love, loneliness and eternity— "lava lamp poetry," I call it, all swirling image without, well, *thrust*. But I was apparently a minority opinion: When she was done, Rose got a standing ovation.

"I want to read one more poem," she said when the applause died down.

"Only one?" someone complained.

Rose blushed more. "It's dedicated to my friend Abner, who taught me a lot this summer about being a poet and a friend."

I didn't know it was coming. "Food is the Drug of the Jews," she said, and read it in a tremulous voice.

I reproduce it here:

Food is the drug of the Jews.
They are not a happy people like the Irish,
whose daughter I am. They do not drink,
but wandering has made them hungry.

They love to eat, but I have noticed
something strange: they don't get full.

Food doesn't make them happy.
What kind of drug is that?

When Irish drink, we sing and can forget.
But Jews are cursed with memory
of something more sweet to them than food:
a chosen place called Home to eat it in.

Food is no drug at all, no food
can sate the longing to go home to eat.
Thank you for teaching me this mystery of
wandering.
Hunger, not food, is the drug of the Jews.

I joined the bravos, tears starting in my eyes for the gift of the poem, for its small cargo of truth and for the remembrance of my homelessness and loneliness. Yes, the Wandering Jew made a nice counterpoint to Gauguin.

Triumphant at the lectern, Rose beamed above the audience at me; yet I read sadness in her face as well and felt a tremendous closeness to her. The summer's two months of hard cultivation of plants and poetry had borne the best fruit: We were friends. At that moment, weighted with the imminence of saying goodbye, I would have done anything for her.

"This is your going-away party, I guess," Mars suggested beside me. He laid a brotherly hand on my shoulder.

"I miss you already, old friend," I told him. I threw my arm around him and we embraced.

Over Mars's shoulder, I saw Rose, hostess manqué, bustling cakes out of the kitchen, moving in a circle of friends, gesturing, smiling, licking her fingers, enjoying her celebrity. She would live among these people differently now, they knew her in a changed way. Again she caught my eye and waved gaily. My arm around Mars, I signaled back. I already missed her too.

The last guests were gone. Mars had taken home the new lady he was courting and would be back. Alone in the house, Rose and I cleared paper plates into trash bags, sponged the tabletops, replaced the furniture. The house was big and echoey, and I felt, as we did the mundane chores, a rising consciousness of being alone with her. Perhaps she felt the same, for the conversation lapsed and we grew quiet, sensitive to one another's presence, almost shy.

Rose was a woman whose physical presence I had catalogued and dismissed many times before: a round face, broad shoulders, small breasts, unmanageable and mousey brown hair, dressed on a daily basis in sensible shoes, unfeminine jeans and loose shirts that hid her and made her look heavy.

She looked different to me now. The long dark skirt modeled her hips as she walked, so that (the poet's eye obscenely seeing) I imagined the dark and light of her thighs moving beneath. Her hair, brushed out, fell in dark waves onto her shoulders, over the white blouse, shadowing her breasts. Wearing makup and scent, she seemed grown up, a woman risen, no messy adolescent. Her eyes were bright, filled with the pleasure of tonight's success.

I, too, felt born anew. My body was slimmed and muscular. I too wore finery purchased especially for this night: a forest-green tunic and brown pants, loose cotton garments that felt good against my skin. Garbed in the colors of the earth, I was a figure in a medieval pageant—the Troubadour. Yes, Victorian Rose and I, lord and lady of this manor tonight, might well play roles in a mythic tale of our own devising.

Thus physical lust clothes itself in metaphysicals.

And why not, I thought, why not?

We are sitting on the living room floor with cups of tea on a low table between us. The cleanup is done and we are tired. The house is quiet. Rose is chewing her bottom lip in a worried way.

"Peter didn't call?" I suggest.

She shakes her head, then shrugs.

"Does Peter like your poems?"

She shrugs again. "He reads them, but he doesn't usually say anything about them."

"Maybe he's not the poetry type."

"He's the Reality Principle type," she says. She looks up at me and we smile.

I could put my hand over hers, I think to myself, or slide my finger briefly against her finger. But I am savoring thc moment; there is no rush. Outside are the woods, the ocean cliffs, the enormous star-filled sky. I wonder what Rose is thinking as her ten fingers unconsciously makes a small tent on the table. I take it for a symbol of vulnerability and of protection. Something is beginning. Perhaps Rose is waiting for it no less than I.

In the silence, I think about Rose in her own life: Roman Catholic upbringing, retarded sister, fear of abandonment, restauranteur and poet, cold Peter, an apprehension of childlessness.

When I look again at her, she has not moved, except a tear is crawling slowly down her cheek. It is the only detail of movement in the room. Rose is weeping for herself. I feel a thrill inside me.

I say her name gently. "Rose?" Another tear falls. She turns her face away, then gets up and goes to the mantle to get a tissue and stands there, turned away.

At other times I have prided myself on restraint—that I could have touched but did not, allowing a scene to evolve on its own, more faithful to it than to my own desire, enjoying anticipation more than action. But this time I want her, as a woman and as a friend. I will be leaving in two days; I do not know what will happen in my life after that. A poem will not be enough for us to remember each other by. *He who desires but acts not breeds pestilence—*

I went to her and put my hand on her shoulder. She turned, her face softened with weeping. "Rose," I said again, and I gently brushed away the tear on her cheek with my finger. I put my fingertip to my lip, tasting her sadness, accepting it into me. So close together in the empty house, we looked into each other's eyes. In that arena of decision, I waited to be overcome, for the wings of joy-as-it-flies to lift and carry me. I breathed the air, feeling the power of her close human presence, and then leaned down to kiss her. She partly turned her face, giving me a corner of her mouth. "Abner—"

I cupped her cheek, then held up my hand. "Friends?" I proposed.

"Friends," she agreed, and put her palm against mine. I kissed her fingers, clasping them against the little tug she made to get them back. I thought to myself that I had not noticed before how blue and clear her eyes were.

And then the rush of it came with new intensity, and I put my hands on her shoulders, drew her to me and kissed her fully, wanting her. She said my name again, said no, pushed at me—and yet she kissed me back, and I heard the woman-sound deep in her throat. "Rose"—my hands were pulling her against me, wanting her. She was pushing me away and yet her mouth kept coming back to mine. In a moment, I felt, she would melt against me, her No dissolving into Yes, her mouth against my ear and her hands on me. Friendship, lust, a desire to be master of this house—inflamed, I breathed her name into her ear, stroked her long hair. My hands investigated her flanks, I felt the side of her breast against my thumb, I pressed her against me. "No," she moaned, pushing weakly back, "oh, Abner, no, please, Abner—." Somewhere far away, a car pulled into the driveway outside: Mars coming back. My hand cupped the white cloth over her breast, my fingers reached through the buttons to feel her bare skin. "Abner, no—"

The door opened and closed. A moment later a voice, puzzled, at the living room threshhold, not angry, only confused: "What's going on here? Rose?" It was Peter.

We broke apart—I let her go and stepped back, Peter a dark presence by the door, my eyes still attentive to Rose. She stepped away from me, her face flushed with effort and the rubbing of my skin against hers, her loose hair and white blouse disheveled.

"What's going on here?" Peter said again, more sternly, moving into the situation to take control. Rose took several steps away from me, toward him, making it clear that I had forced myself on her, that she was his.

Peter glanced at her briefly, then his eyes swung back to me. "What the *hell* is going on?" he said belligerently, understanding it now. "Rose?" He glanced at her, and she came toward him, hands half raised in a gesture of surrender. Her mouth moved, but no sounds came out. I am your victimized ally, she wanted to tell him, assuring him that none of this had been her idea, that I had betrayed them both.

He turned to me again, took another step toward me. He said, "Get out of here, Abner—get out." I felt the heat on my cheeks, felt my clothes uncomfortably awry—my shirt half pulled out of my pants, my pants twisted on my waist. And I felt furious to be interrupted, so angry to be made subordinate again that the tautness of guilt fell away, and I met his eyes fully, hating him for having come back and for taking away what I wanted and could, I thought, have had. Somehow, I felt years full of reasons for hating him. "Fuck you, Peter," I told him madly. "Just go fuck yourself."

He took three more steps, closing the space between us. "Rose is mine," he informed me conversationally and slapped me a sudden backhand across the face, knocking me sideways, hurting me. The blow reverberated in the bone of my skull, and humiliated tears came into my eyes, not so much for the pain as for the contemptuousness of the delivery—backhand, not even a punch. I took it not merely as an attack but as a challenge.

Behind Peter, Rose said *his* name now, pleading; neither of us paid her any attention.

Something was in the way of what I wanted, as if the stump had been replanted in my heart. As if all my work had been undone. Rage filled me. Not on account of Rose, whom I dismissed now, for I knew I would never have her, even as I decided to fight for her. But I would not accept losing, I would not acquiesce in having nothing.

A growling sound began in my throat as I threw myself against him, punching and pummelling. I wanted to hit his face, to smash his self-satisfied face until he surrendered. I wanted to get my hands around his throat.

My first blows landed on his body and forced him back. (In some other world, I heard Rose shouting, "Peter, no! Peter! Peter!") He sidestepped my wild attack, and as I came back at him, he used both hands to slap me again three times, hard, across my face—crack! crack! crack!

Over Rose's voice I heard my own scream of rage as I tried to get at him. But I was no fighter, and he eluded me. After my first blows, he hit me open-handed time after time, dancing back from my fists, and when I would not give up—though my nose bled and tears of frustration and pain half blinded me—he stepped into me.

As if I were watching it in slow motion, I saw the choreography. Some distant part of me could admire Peter's matador grace as he sidestepped and punched, catching me on the side of the head, on the chest and then with the full force of his forearm on the back of my head so that I stumbled and fell hard onto the floor with my arm underneath me.

"Don't get up again," he instructed, breathing hard. "I'll beat the living shit out of you."

"Peter, *please*"—Rose again, pulling at him. He brushed her away, cold and certain, staring down at me. I scrabbled, trying to get up. It would be better to be beaten to pulp than to let him walk away from me lying on the floor. I struggled up dizzily, the pain of the fall in my side, wiping blood off my mouth. *Let him kill me*, I thought, *but he won't win.* If I could hurt him, I would not be defeated.

"Don't be an asshole, Abner," he said.

Half shut down to some inner elemental animal nature that could endure pain and battle, I managed a lopsided erectness and stared at him, panting like a bull, appraising the enemy; and then I attacked, aiming for his face again, wanting to see his blood too.

He blocked me and struck, this time with his fists—my cheek, the side of my eye, once over the heart and once, hard, in the stomach, so that food came up sickeningly into my mouth. I lunged, and he hit me again, banging me back against the wall. I slid down onto the floor again, into that twilight where animals go to nurse themselves or die. . . .

When I opened my eyes dully, they were both looking down at me, Rosie weeping silently, her hand in her mouth, Peter's dark face cold and expressionless. After my first flurry, I knew I had not landed a single blow.

"Peter? Rosie?" Someone else was at the doorway looking in. For some reason, I noted clearly that he called her Rosie instead of Rose. "Is everything all right? Oh, my goodness," he cried, seeing me on the floor. I focused on him: a balding fellow with glasses and a fleshy, clean face; he looked like a comical accountant in a television sitcom, like the young Phil Silvers. I understood without interest that this was Barry—Big Bucks. "My goodness," he said again, peering around the door-post but not coming in. "What happened?"

No one answered him. Almost immediately, Mars, returned from his lady friend, pushed past him into the room. He was already moving toward me when Peter said, "See about him, will you, Mars." They were all looking down at me in the darkened room—

Al is in town and staying with us. When I come home from a late class, they do not hear me enter the darkened front room. From where I stand, I can see into the bright kitchen. The four of them are arranged around the table, talking and passing bowls of food: Al, Lora, Eli, Ella—Mom, Dad, Buddy and Sis—someone else's family. I feel I have blundered into the wrong house and stand in the shadows like an intruder, watching their family together at dinner. I am a kind of photographer, seeing everything but out of the picture, one step removed—stepfather, stephusband, stepman.

I saw Peter take Rose's hand and lead her away. Big Bucks

followed after them. Mars put a comforting hand on my shoulder, got ice for the swelling, helped me to the couch. Where would I escape to now? "You want to go to India, man?" I asked, holding the ice against my cheek.

I must have looked pretty awful, for tears brimmed in Mars's eyes as he looked down at me. "There is no India, man," he said at last.

"No India?" I joked, holding off hurt. "What about for Indians?"

"Especially not for Indians," said Mars.

CHAPTER 17

On the long road east, I got stopped twice by cops in small towns for no reason. Maybe my bruised face made me look like a thug, and they wanted to check me out. Poet as Thug. Maybe they were right—I could have been someone fleeing the scene of a crime.

"I'm sorry," she had said the next day. It was late in the morning when I finally made my bruised way downstairs. I thought no one was home, but she was in the garden, weeding the tomatoes, those ripening fruits I would not get to taste. As I watched her through the window—dressed again in her work jeans, a baggy shirt, sensible shoes—it was hard to believe she had been the object of last night's passion. Somehow her plainness aggravated my feeling of shame toward her and then my anger at her for having shamed me.

She must have stayed at home to wait for me, for when she saw me at the window, she came into the house, wanting to talk. I suppose she felt that half pitiful, half noble woman's need to try to make everything be all right again.

She was sorry about what had happened, she said, sorry for our misunderstanding, very sorry about the fight. You look awful, she told me with a sympathetic laugh; then her eyes misted over. She said she wanted to know how I felt, wanted me to know how much she valued talking with me all summer, confiding in me, having me for a poetry buddy and a friend. "I did want to be your friend," she said. "I *do*."

It was sincere, I think. It was also her prepared goodbye, and by the time she changed paragraphs, I had stopped listening. All that mattered about the summer was already inside me. The reality was not what had happened, Cyna told me, but what I would make out of it. Rose was already drifting into the past.

I watched her mouth move for a few moments more, then I told her not to worry about it and went back upstairs.

I took the rest of the day to recuperate and pack. In the afternoon, with help from Mars, I layered my gear into the back of my station wagon. Peter had been gone all day, and I took some satisfaction from the notion, even though it did not seem likely, that he might be avoiding me. Does the Reality Principle feel discomfort about its victims? I doubted it, but I was glad not to have to face him.

Late that afternoon, I booked a room in a motel. No more Peter, no more Rose. Mars—my old friend, oldest friend, connection to my cowboy dreamer past—bought me dinner in town. Our conversation was all reminiscence and farewell. Afterward, we drove back to the motel and parked his pickup next to my Plymouth. The night was clear, the sky full of distant stars, with that panoramic bigness the Western sky sometimes boasts. So we sat together in the dark of the front seat, saying final goodbyes, calling up the old covenant of brotherhood between us, knowing we would meet again but not knowing when. "Mars—" I said then, blurting the thought I had decided not to say, "man, I have to ask you—What are you *doing* living there?"

He paused and gave me his sideways glance, insulted, I saw, by the trace of scorn that had leaked into my voice. "I live there because I like it there," he said. "What, did you decide they're evil people just because you acted like a shmuck?"

"No," I said, "that's not what I meant." But I couldn't explain what I meant, for it was a harsh judgement that had trickled out, it was Mars's life I was questioning, not theirs. "I just want you to have a place that's *yours*," I told him at last. "You deserve it."

He said nothing. And while we sat those final moments in the darkness, I recalled something I had filed away at the beginning of my visit. Of all the time I had spent with Mars in the past weeks, that first event now seemed to me the essential one, the key.

He had taken me with him in the pickup over back-country roads to visit Roxy in her cabin in the woods. He and Roxy had been lovers, had lived together there. It was over between them now, but Mars wasn't over it.

She was a willowy woman of about thirty, an old-style country hippie in a long peasant skirt, with streaky brown-blonde hair falling down into her face. She came out onto the steps of the cabin when we drove up, but extended only a faint, unsmiling hello. Mars pretended not to notice that she wasn't glad to see him.

Her three kids, however, boys about ten and eight and a girl around five, were delighted for him to be there, and he, barging inside, played favorite uncle with them, letting them sit on his lap and climb onto his shoulders while he told them crazy stories and looked at their treasures. Roxy did not offer us food or drink and, though Mars made himself at home, she never actually invited us to sit down. I saw in her face the bitter exhaustion she would confront after we left, the painful work of putting back together the emotional fragments of her household and dealing all by herself with her children, who wanted Mars for a father.

I knew a lot of that first hand, from how Lora and I each felt after visits from Al when Eli and Ella were small. But this was worse. Roxy was alone, for one thing, and something about her passive silence and the dark messiness of the cabin communicated depression and incapacity. After we left, I thought, she just might not have reserves to give. She might merely ignore the broken pieces, leave the kids alone to work it out for themselves. Boisterous now, they might have no help or comfort with the emotional distress that, in who knew what disguise, would end up defining them as adults.

"I'll come visit again," Mars said as we left. Roxy only nodded faintly and still said nothing. But when the kids kept hanging onto Mars's legs, wanting him to stay, she spoke sharply to them. They finally let go and stood quiet, the little one with her thumb in her mouth, to watch us climb back in the truck.

As we drove the country roads back to Peter and Rose's, Mars heaved heavy sighs behind the steering wheel. Finally, voice full of grief, he explained. "I don't know what happened," he said. "I loved her. I loved those kids. I would drive down there after work, or wait till Saturday and go for the weekend. I'd been working all week, I wanted to kick back, read the Sunday comics to the kids, putter around, make love. I thought we were having fun. She finally told me she hated being so domestic."

She should have taken him, I thought, for her kids' sake as well as for hers. But she had wanted someone to take her away from being housewife and mother, not somebody else to take care of.

After they broke up, Mars had moved from his room in town into the house with Rose and Peter. "You know what I realized?" he challenged me. "I realized I just didn't want to be *alone* any more."

Was that a weakness, to want not to be alone? Sitting in his pickup in the motel parking lot, I wondered if Mars was what people meant when they said someone is a failure: a little restaurant work, a little hauling, his bed a mattress on the floor in somebody else's house, not having figured out what his life was for and who would go along with him on the journey. Thirty-five years old and still trying to patch a life together.

And if Mars was a failure, I thought now, driving east into the blinding sun, what did that make me?

And so the long return. The country as I drove it seemed so huge, so *unnecessarily* big. Heading for the denouement of my own story, I didn't need all this space between me and the next part of my life.

Stopping only to eat and sleep, I drove from early morning, with the air still cool and the sun like a needle in my eye, till late in the afternoon, sweltering in the August heat, my elongated shadow stretched out before me on the highway. It was as if the self-punishment of the driving liberated mind from body. The road ran straight across the country. Feeling like a machine inside a machine, I let my mind chart its own course.

This (I thought) has been my poverty: All I ever owned or cared about were my feelings and experience, but I had never known exactly where they led or what to do with them. Is this the sad estate of the poet only or the general condition? ("Imprisoned in the personal/ like honey in a glass of tea." Ah, Rose!)

I had no safe theories to parallel the scientist's, the scholar's or the priest's, no paradigms, no certainties of knowledge, no way to make sense of the world except through experience and feelings. Choosing the only way I knew to understanding, then, I retold my story to myself as I drove.

From the first images of the world of flesh, grainy memories of bedtime and my mother's face, I recalled the foreign continent of childhood: myself at five and at ten, a fat boy alien and dissatisfied in my family's dark rooms, growing private fantasies of love and freedom—the poet germinating. I remembered my long hours in school, forced to fit, trying hard to please, learning to stand in line like everybody else. I recounted to myself the dramas of puberty and the painful comedies of adolescence, I named to myself the friends of high school and college, now scattered and lost, and counted the women who had introduced me to the second world of flesh and whom I had pursued out of my own great need to be loved. I relived my life with Lora, with Eli and Ella, with my own Hannah, and I recited my poems to myself, remembering my moments of surprised inspiration. Far away in my mind's sad eye, I saw all my little tributaries converge into the river of my adult, formed life as husband, father and teacher; I watched the slow metamorphosis of that little boy called by my name into this man, Abner Minsky—a machine inside a machine on his way to an uncertain rendezvous.

I knew I had made a mess of things. And I still could not see the way out.

If the story were fiction, there would be some transformative epiphany, some change I was heading for. In this, literature and psychology agree, for change is the myth and the marketable commodity of both. The hero's eyes are opened, he overcomes his obstacle, he learns to be or see a new way.

But I, the homeless man on his way home, could not glimpse any change approaching in the blinding sun or feel it dragging me behind it in the long shadow. And so I had to consider the unpalatable possibility that, despite poetry and Mrs. Kramer, there might be no change—that I could simply drive the car, a machine within a machine, and never change at all.

Yes, said I to the smiling ribbon of the American highway, consider this: a man whose personality is so cemented in its place that change is impossible. Consider that there may be no happy ending. Consider Mars. Consider my office mate at Athens College, Fred Petrucelli, that Wordsworth scholar and failed fiction writer, forty years old with a pointy academic goatee and acne-scarred cheeks, a nice guy with a bad self-image. For two years, we have lunched together every Friday, and over hamburgers and salad he has described in fantastic, fascinating detail the particular, peculiar dynamics of his personal life—explaining, categorizing, pinning his problems wriggling on the wall for me, art appreciator in the gallery of his blocked life, to help him understand.

And yet, students, observe: Despite his generous articulation, we see no change, no movement. He only returns each Monday morning untransformed, carrying another morbific, fully documented—well-told!—weekend tale about the lover who will not commit or the one who demands too much, his fat mother's impossible claims on him, the difficulties he encounters in finishing his monograph on Wordsworth. All the tics and tocs of his ambivalence he lays out cleanly on the table between us like a dentist's tools, but he makes no extractions, drills no cavities. He is not even a bore, most of the time, but a cultured man knowing and witty about his agonies—a vulnerable, expressive, loving, *likable* guy and a feeling performer of Wordsworth's poems besides.

But he does not change. A man inadequate to his private ambitions, fettered in chains no thicker than his own thoughts, he is at a third remove: trapped in his situation, trapped in his understanding of his situation and trapped in all his devices for trying to escape his situation. (And after me, I see, he goes on to the next art appreciator, calls in the next listener to hear the day's poor news.) Things happen in his life, but he does not *change*, and colleagues and friends mock him sympathetically, as I am doing.

Fred Petrucelli, friend of failure. And if Fred Petrucelli is a failure, what am I?

For I too can speak of change while choosing what does not nourish me. I too can diagram my preference to burrow into the wrong nest and to become—by my own free choice!—the worker in the wrong job, the lover of the wrong woman, the husband of the wrong wife, the father of the wrong children, even the author of the wrong poems. The second husband, the unsuccessful cuckolder, the rodenty rummager through the strange lady's desk as if it were the lady's silken underpants, trying to see what little puckered residence I might discover there for myself. And all the while never quite slicing off a life that is my own.

But hold a minute, protests the brilliant morning sun. You changed your path in order to be husband, father, happy genius of a household. You fought for it, in fact. Are those changes nothing but despair in disguise?

And hold a moment, insists the soothing penumbra of late afternoon. Aren't you forgetting Love? Love brought you to Lora Sachsman. You loved her and those children. Is that heroic love to be derided now as self-betrayal in disguise?

Love is love, said poet to sun and shadow. I do not apologize for it, but I don't know what it is, either. Here I am, drawn and pulled, a man rolling between two coasts, and all the strenuous changes and choices of my life seem no more real and lasting than the changes made in the sea by waves and tides—cycles; changes of mood. Only a child (or a poet with no real vision) will believe each oscillation as a separate truth.

Freud, engineer of the mind, saw too that a self-destructive man could wearily repeat his pattern over and over, not changing but merely returning again and again, in fresh disguise, to recreate anew the same old painful stew of circumstance. A man might learn to use words about himself and tell the truth, but change nothing essential.

Wordsworth too:

> We poets in our youth begin in gladness;
> But thereof come in the end despondency and
> madness.

Thereof. I had always before somehow overlooked the word "thereof." I had understood merely the sequence of youth and age but not the *causality* of despair. Thereof! The poet trapped from the beginning in the cramped box of the personality! Out of gladness, playfulness, delight in being, desire for knowledge, unstudied love—one makes a mess of things. Out of the glad expectation comes the painful thwarting. One stretches, but the essential Self does not give an inch.

I had dug up the stump, yes, but then I had replanted it in my heart. Or, more precisely, it had been there from the beginning, and even true love and the free soul's outpouring of charm and goodness only brought me back to it again, over and over. No matter how detailed my investigation of my childhood and my past, the dead stump stayed, impossible to uproot, strangling the garden.

So it was in horror of my own personality that I exited the New York Thruway onto local highways. The landscape became gradually more familiar to my eye, until at last I turned onto the well-known windy road that ran down along Ithaca Lake to Athens, New York.

CHAPTER 18

I had driven this winding road along the lake before. The cross-county route from the lake to the Athens crossroads was even more familiar, and then came the turnoff for business traffic—and I was in town. My entire life had passed in front of me and now I was back again in Athens, New York, the drowned man, with nothing resolved.

The streets looked brand new, as if outlines had been drawn around trees, buildings, even the streets and sidewalks themselves. And everything looked totally familiar at the same time. I remembered this Arco station, its convenience-store sign looming above decorative shrubbery when you came down Ithaca Avenue. I remembered the row of shiny fast-food places (and knew the taste of burgers in every one). I recognized like an old friend the lot with broken yellow fencing around it at the corner of Buffalo Street, my cue to turn right. It was like *déja vu.* I had been here before, yet it seemed somehow like a dream.

I, too, was newly outlined, slimmed down and muscular, bruised from my beating, and no different than before.

And now here was the residential street and the red frame house whose lower floor was "home." Like a drifter, I parked across the street and sat in the car, watching it. Beyond the curtains on the big front window—curtains Lora had made of fabric we had chosen together—was the life I had fled two months before.

Enter the uncertain second husband at his door.

And here is Lora, at once most familiar and most foreign. Her hair is pulled back. Her face is freshly washed. Dressed in bluejeans and a print blouse, she looks like a 1950s schoolgirl. She has a cool half smile on her face. She has been expecting me, of course, but she does not know what to expect.

My wife and I have our way when we meet after a separation. As if we have entered into the realm of ritual, we do not touch. We keep a distance first, becoming reacquainted. We are reluctant to intrude or assume too much.

So we said hello and looked at one another. We gave each other an awkward sibling hug.

"How are you?"

"Fine. And you?"

"Fine."

"How's Hannah?"

"Also fine. She's in daycare and looking forward to seeing you."

I nodded and stepped into my home. Looking around, I followed Lora through the living room to the dining area, where Lora's parents, my in-laws Bernie and Bea, rose from the table to welcome me.

I knew they would be there, of course, informed by Lora when I had called to fine-tune my time of arrival. They were on their way back from their annual trip to Florida and had stayed an extra day to "see me." This made me expect, as we all sat down again after the effusion of greetings, that I was in for some sort of family powwow.

But it never happened. They asked questions about my trip, inquired after Mars, whom they knew from our previous life in California. They clucked to me over how wonderful Hannah was, bigger and smarter every day, and about Eli and Ella, whom they had seen at Al's house on their way north—bright, attractive, creative, "mature." Bernie and I talked about transcontinental road conditions; Bea reminisced about their motor trips to Yosemite and the Grand Canyon. Neither of them said: "How come you went on a vacation by yourself?" Or: "Are you planning to divorce Lora?" Or: "Can we talk about the difficulties and strains that you are encountering in your family life?" None of that. Instead, we had food.

My in-laws had kindly imported "appetizing" in a cooler all the way from Miami Beach—smoked salmon, whitefish and lox, definitely not the kind you get prepackaged at an upstate supermarket—and they had even more kindly saved some of it for my arrival. While we talked, Lora unfolded the greasy white paper around the appetizing and dealt out paper plates. Bea sliced up a cucumber and tomatoes. "Would you put up water, Abner?" Lora asked politely.

Yes, that is something I know how to do in this dwelling place. The metal teapot is an inarticulate but intimate old friend that shines with the gloss of all the times I have breakfasted here, or procrastinated a project with a cup of coffee, or prepared cups of tea for an evening chat with Lora. We have shared many events, this utilitarian pot with its comfortable black plastic grip and I. Hearing its shrill whistle, I know my special kinship with it.

I bring the teapot to the table and pour water into cups. We settle into the food. Every once in a while, as we eat the salty fish and talk our ordinary family talk, I get from Lora a knowing eyeball, of whose meaning I am not certain. I guess she is feeling the oddness of our contactless reunion and meanwhile coping energetically with the strain of three days with her parents.

My father-in-law is a small man who sports a Don Ameche mustache and a blue polyester leisure suit. Retired now, he earned his living as a small-appliance dealer, is still loyal to Zenith and is willing to tell you why. Bernie had more in common with Al, another gadget lover and machine repairer, than he does with me, even though Al's lifestyle and philosophy gave him heartburn. Poetry is alien, a subject that does not interest him. He *likes* me well enough, I suppose, but how can a down-to-earth, practical guy like him comprehend a man like me, who thinks writing poems is a serious career? I would bet it was not his idea to stay longer in Athens in order to see me.

Mother Bea, on the other hand, is a warm Jewish mama with a nose for news. Having just returned from visiting Lora's older brother Arnie in Florida, she enlivens our tabletalk with tales of her daughter-in-law (that's Lora's brother Arnie's wife, my sister-in-law Phoebe), with whom she has been feuding for twenty years, ever since she interfered in Phoebe's choice of wedding gowns. Bea is a meddler, all right, but since meddling is a form of poetry, I like listening to her stories, even with their refrain of self-justification. "All I *said* was," she exclaims, or "*All* I did was"—as in, "All I *did* was, because I knew she wouldn't fit into the dress she bought for Rosh Hashanah, was I suggested that she shouldn't feel like she *has* to eat cake at every meal. Is that so terrible?" She turns an innocent hand up, not recollecting all the times Phoebe has screamed at her to stop nagging her about being fat.

"Did you bring cake when you went to visit?" Lora asks.

"Well, I couldn't come in empty-handed, could I?" Bea replies, looking at me.

"You couldn't," I agree. Lora and I share a knowing smile. "This stuff sure is wonderful," I say, licking a greasy finger, and the conversation meanders back to appetizing. New York appetizing is the best. Even this Miami Beach appetizing is not as good. You just can't get appetizing like New York appetizing anywhere in the world. "Not even Israel," says Bea, shaking her head in sympathy for the Jewish state. She recalls the time they went for appetizing in Tel Aviv, how dirty the restaurant was and how it all tasted Moroccan. Reminded of foreign spices, she wrinkles her nose.

Did they really want to see me? In order to talk this trivial family talk? Well, yes, it could be: I am their son-in-law, they wanted to see me and to talk trivial family talk. I always expect depths of meaning, but Bea likes appetizing. She likes to have her family around her. Her and Bernie's ambition for this visit was, like them, not deep—to eat and gossip and be a family. Why can't I relax and be a family with them? What infernal pride makes me cringe at living ordinary life?

We stood out in front of the house, watching Bernie and Bea's car till it turned toward the highway. I let the personal sun warm my face. We were alone. "So?" she said. "You lost weight." She paused, peering at me. "I didn't even really look at you yet. Your face is kind of—Did you hurt yourself?"

"I ran into a door," I said. It was the truth, metaphorically speaking. "How was your summer?"

"I got a lot done. You can get a lot done when nobody's around," she added. "I got offered a one-woman show at the Downtown Gallery—"

"That's great."

"And I started doing a children's book—I'll show you later—"

"Good."

"—And I managed to frame a lot of my old drawings, and the people at the bookstore said they would be willing to hang them and try to sell them."

"That's great."

"It's been a good summer," she said. She paused. "My parents are worried about us, you know."

"They didn't act worried."

"They talked to me before you came. They asked me if they should have a talk with you. My mom told me I should shave my legs and under my arms."

I laughed. "She's been trying to get you to do that for years."

"Yeah, but this time she hinted it might be the cause of any problems we might be having."

"So are you going to do it?"

"No," said Lora flatly, "I'm not. I want to go inside," she added immediately, as if she had just remembered something important.

I followed her back into the house.

The house was very clean—empty, all mess of children put away, just quiet, a restful inwardness. The genital paintings on the living room walls had been replaced by a series of gentle collages.

Lora busied herself putting things away from the meal, apparently ignoring me. I wandered into my office. My typewriter crouched under its heavy cloth cover, made for me by Lora three birthdays ago; my good brown desk stood patiently under a patina of dust; my books still lodged heavily on their shelves. In my absence, however, Lora had moved into my room Hannah's box of blocks and another box of toys and books that Hannah was too old for now. A braided area rug that had been in our bedroom was rolled up against the wall, and rolled beside it were the genital paintings, waiting to be stored. One part of my study seemed to have become a closet for overflow.

When I went to investigate, I saw that Lora had cleared out a section of our (our?) bedroom, in order to expand her workspace. Her two-tiered painting cart stood there now, filled with squeezed tubes of acrylic paint Stapled on the wall beside it were a series of new paintings-in-progress: small colored circles and triangles tumbling over each other, like blind symbolic women and men.

Beside these, a little table stacked with blank sheets of newsprint and a chair—a painting station for Hannah. I remembered, as if from long ago, my wife's good ideas and happy energies, her desire for us to live always surrounded by bright colors, a family of artists.

There were a couple of other changes here, too. In the corner, on a milk crate next to the bed, was a battered black-and-white TV, its antenna raised in a V-for-Victory sign. Mostly at my insistence, we had kept television out of the house, despite Eli's and Ella's lobbying. But the house had been hers for the summer, with no husband to negotiate lifestyle changes with or adolescent children to protect or defend against. I wondered if the TV would stay now.

The calm, quiet house seemed more hers than mine.

I was used to having final leverage, to being the one who would accept or reject our life together. How many times, acknowledging the imbalance, had Lora wistfully sighed, "I need you more than you need me, I love you more than you love me."

But what, I thought, if Lora was freed of her role in our melodrama, poor Nell no more? What if she had learned to get along just fine by herself? For one moment, unbraced from our complicated harness, I saw Lora, secure and autonomous, wanting nothing from me—and felt the surge of panic.

She was sitting at the table kitchen, writing in her journal, the private person hard at work. I felt the primitive urge to possess—her breast in my hand, my hands on her, myself inside her. "I'm going to take a shower," I said. She looked at me sideways and nodded.

Under the cascade of hot water, I lathered myself in private places and contemplated her hands on me. Afterward, pulling on clean clothes, I felt ready for several kinds of wrangling with my wife—I felt almost happy, somehow, as if water and the ambition to fuck my wife had cured me, made me once more capable of thrust.

But when I emerged—of course!—Lora's face was set against me, darkly infused with a hurt of her own. She walked past and did not look at me.

"Is something wrong?"

"No," she said, not stopping. But yes, I recognized the old dynamic. Our sudden opposition of needs, this miniature but telling shift in the climate, was just what *happened* between us. It was our private hydroponics germinating the larger misunderstandings of our life together. And yet, at the same time, it was somehow the proof of the indelible link between us. Through the humid air and closed door of the bathroom, Lora had sensed what I was conscious of only in its coarsest manifestation—the need to be joined with her. This need turned around in her, made her feel invaded; thus she retreated. For two months, she had been alone, able to paint and organize her space and life, but now I was back and things were about to get messy again, in all senses of the word.

Full of understanding, I went back to fold and hang the damp towels neatly on the rack.

I found her mixing paints, resuming her private life. I said, "We have to talk."

"Okay," she said in a neutral tone, as if she had been waiting for me. She recapped the tube of cobalt blue.

I made tea and we sat at the kitchen table, as in former times, fiddling with the spoons and teabags, "having a talk," but not yet talking, looking at each other across the table.

"So?" Lora said at last.

"So," I said. "I'm back."

"You're back," she agreed. "I noticed. Did you have a good summer? Are you ready to write about what you did on your summer vacation?"

I appealed to Cyna to help me say something honest, something I had not said before—something real to break through the brittleness.

"Did you sleep with anyone while I was gone?" I blurted. It had been on my mind since California, the scariest question I could think of the answer to—the matter of possession. Exclusivity—"faithfulness"—was the oldest and most urgent of all the agreements on which our life together was based, pledged far back in the early days. I had been willing to betray it. Had she taken the same freedom I had tried to grab for myself?

"No," she said and looked at me like I was nuts. Then something dawned. "*You* did?"

"No, I didn't," I said quickly, staring right back at her.

"You're sure," she persisted.

"Absolutely," I told her, then changed course. "I was just worried about you."

She nodded, satisfied, apparently willing to take my suspicion as a compliment, not an admission. It had been awkward, but perhaps I had used the right mechanism after all, for the stiffness between us was broken, the moment entered into. "You look well," she said appraisingly. "You're thin, you have a tan. You also have unexplained *bruises* on your face," she added in her Bronx raven's voice.

I shrugged. "Eli and Ella are okay?"

"Eli and Ella are fine. Hannah is fine. I'm fine. I guess everything is fine." She shot me a glance. "Are you back for good, Abner? Why don't we just get down to it. Are we still married, Abner? Are you my husband?"

Right to the point; Minsky could have danced for days. And now the answer, please, maestro? After all, any intentions were honorable, if I would state them honestly.

I didn't know the answer. Was Husband back for good?

I knew about being married to Lora, the disappointments of friendship, the stale smell of failure mixed with love. I knew I didn't have the energy for another mauling break with the past. There was nowhere else I wanted to go—I had nowhere else *to* go. So, yes, I wanted to stay. Perhaps that was the same as wanting to be Lora's husband?

Across the table, Lora watched me, her expression guarded, waiting for me to decide our lives. I knew the corners of that mouth, the slope of her neck, I knew the taste of those ears and eyes—I knew the landscape of Lora, body and soul. And as I watched, lust—yes, the pure vector of it—bloomed and blossomed again inside me. Warm blood came rippling to the surfaces of my skin. Bless lust: Intention focused, one knows what one wants.

So in that moment, I desired to repossess my life. "Yes," I said, my voice confessional. "Yes, Lora, I want to be your husband."

For the lie was true. Don't you see, it was as simple as meaning: I wanted to be husband to my wife. Isn't that what she had asked?

You might say I had compromised both honesty and ambition, that I had failed once again as poet and cowboy hero. Shrug. At that moment, it was the best I could do.

She let me take her hand across the table, then withdrew. As at other times, I wondered if she could read my mind, for she said, "Did you really answer my question, Abner? I'm not talking about fucking. Either be married to me or go find the wife you really want. I don't want to start all over again with the same bullshit. You were supposed to decide if you want to be married to me. You were supposed to decide if you forgive me. *Just don't waste my time, okay?*"

Tears were in her eyes. Anger and love, anger and love. She must have thought these words many times during the summer. "You have a real tendency to waste my time," she repeated accusatorily, as an afterthought, and for some reason that made her smile through the tears.

And so, old enemies and lovers, we sat across the kitchen table with cups of tea before us, tears in our eyes as we resumed the complicated and difficult negotiation of our lives.

CHAPTER 19

Once—and not long ago, either—at the end of one of our bitter episodes, Lora had stood with tears running down her face and begged, "Forgive me! Abner, please, whatever I did or you think I did, you have to let it go and forgive me!" But I, choking, had fled instead to my notebook, where I had written with trembling fingers words which I could not bring myself to say aloud: *Forgive you? I can't forgive myself for not divorcing you.*

Now, as I sat across the table from her, I remembered that time, and also another time:

Soon after we had moved to Athens, Ella, about eleven years old then, had entered a phase of totally hating Eli. She demonized him, blaming him for everything that went wrong in her life. She accused him of bullying her, of talking for her, of taking her things without asking, of acting self-righteous and all-knowing. She claimed that he stole her friends away from her but would never include her with his friends. Because of him, she said, she had nothing and no one. His existence was in itself a provocation.

One night, so fully of fury she could hardly move, unable even to cry, she lay, hot and dry with hatred, pronouncing her bitter indictments against him while I sat beside her on her bed in the dark of her room. Eli, meanwhile, was at a sleepover party, eating pizza and playing computer games. When she finished her litany, I told her, calmly truthful, that even if she was right, even if Eli was a monster, he was out with friends, innocent to himself, having a good time; she was the one at home with venom in her heart. It was her own feelings, not Eli's wickedness, she had to grapple with.

Why do you speak to me? asked the wise man. Rather speak to yourself.

I knew there would be no full restoration of the kind Lora and I had managed in our early days, forgiveness so deep that we felt born anew. That was a song of innocence, and I was too injured by experience to expect ever to sing it again. Complete healing was for younger men.

But I had to find a way of going on from here. I had to do something. I could not live as this attenuated membrane, so thinned out by anger that all resilience and resonance was gone, capable only of this constant shrill vibration. A whole life could pass away in anger, in dark brooding, and I had no other life to live.

Even if it was Lora's fault, it was my failure.

And there was no one else but her to ask for help.

Goodbye the cowboy hero, fallen in the dust. Goodbye, the American icon. I could not bear to start all over again with nothing. I could not make it on my own, and I was more tired of myself than of anything else.

"What happened to your face?" Lora asked again.

"I got in a fight," I told her. "My face found out I'm in trouble."

"I could have told you that," she said. "In fact, I *did* tell you that."

"Lora, listen. I want to try again. I want us to forgive each other. I want to be home." I hear a dizzy wind rushing in my ears, the words are so hard to say.

I think she knows I am expressing a hope—that is, something not so different from a lie. But because Lora has never stopped loving me, she accepts my words as truth. This is her great strength, that is her power over me.

"Are you asking me to forgive you?" she says quietly. "If you want to be with me, then I forgive you. But make sure Abner. That's all I ask. Just be sure that want you me. *Me*." She pauses. "That *you* forgive *me*."

She is willing to resume our marriage. Really, I can't understand how she can continue to love me. It does not seem to have to do with how I act, with what I give her, with any condition or reward. There is something godlike about it: She loves, she is willing to forgive and to start over. Is she stupid?

But that is her power, that she will always love, always have hope, always be willing to forgive. "That's what I want," I tell her, choked up. "I want to forgive you—"

"Why can't you just *do* it?" she cries. "Just let it go. What are you holding *onto* it for?"

She is right. Why don't I just throw it away and be transformed? As I forgive, I see the past gathered into darkness, and I am bathed in new light.

Yes, that must be possible. But history is real; nothing changes so fast. Nothing changes at all. The forgiveness of which I am capable does not redeem the past, it only endorses the present. The rooted stump remains, defining the garden.

Yet I felt at peace in that moment. I could have sat there forever, for in the vessel of this moment, I had everything I wanted: her attention, her silence, a hope for the future. Once I started to think, all my disappointments and angers would flood in again—if I even moved, the complex patterns of stress would reveal themselves and I would be back in my life with Lora, fighting, worrying, striving, cursing my fate.

I wanted to be home. I wanted to forgive and go on. Going on is not the same as starting over, but that was all the forgiveness I could offer. "You're a damaged person, Abner"—She did not say it, but I saw it again in her cool, accepting eyes. She is right: I am a damaged person.

Lora, if you love me, wait for me.

I place the end of my finger against the end of her finger, like an in-flight refueling. She looks at me. Her face is smooth, dressed with calm. She looks like someone who knows something serious and is amused by it. She looks, actually, quite pretty. She accepts my hand around hers, allows me to touch her hand to my cheek—faint remembered scent of Lora. I am back; she is my wife. We sit there, getting used to it, and then, standing up, making the awkward transition to the other room.

Now I have touched between her legs, have sniffed the talisman of that warm and hairy place. I have towered above her with an erection so big just seeing it made her groan and squirm against the covers.

Beside her in our bed, I remark to myself how small she is; the distance from ankle to knee is so small, so short the bone inside, from knee to hip. How small and vulnerable, the human creature.

Lora's skin is darker than I remembered, her breasts fuller, the V of pubic hair a wilder growth. I think I had imagined the Lora of ten years before, not this mature and womanly matron, half done with her life.

Her knees part for me.

"Come in me," she whispers, and I stroke her open.

And so I re-enter in slow grandeur these silky tunnels of pleasure. We have the perfect fit.

In her eyes, as always, I see myself reflected.

And this is what I want, this that I want to possess, this that

I want to be, this is it at last, a single flesh thrashing and crying out together, me coming coming coming inside her—

This is the high point. Afterward is the coming down, the spent return to everyday reality, the trying to make it all work out.

Penis erectus be my emblem; limp cock, wrinkled and subsided, is my metaphor.

And so we lie with each other, her head upon my arm. My fingers play with her hair, I touch her breast and the soft skin of her arm. We are both thinner than before, both tanned; her skin is smoother than I remember. It is almost as if we are new lovers.

Speech after long silence. She tells me stories of Hannah, of Eli and Ella, of herself. I tell her of Mars, of the journey there and back, of me. We lie quiet, thinking of our separate lives and our life together.

At last I rise from our bed and begin again to put on the garments of my life.

Now we are back in normal time: a trip to the bathroom for Lora, some wandering around the rooms for me. My clothing is in the drawers, my books on the shelves. This is my address.

My alertness to details is accentuated. When I stop in the kitchen and take the orange juice out of the bright mouth of the refrigerator, I notice that we have a new pitcher. I am somehow alarmed to find that something permanent, if trivial, has changed in my absence—it is a sign that things can go on satisfactorily without me.

"You got a new pitcher," I call inanely to Lora.

"Yeah, the old one broke," she calls back.

It is a nice pitcher. I am suspicious of it now, but I know that soon I will not remember the old pitcher which it replaced.

On my desk, in the pile of junk mail and announcements, is a letter from the Dean of Faculty of Athens College, inviting me to the first meeting of the school year.

Another letter informs me that several tenure-track lines are being opened in the Writing Program. I may soon have the opportunity to hold forever the job I don't want at all.

This too is part of the deal.

For the rolled-up nude paintings, Lora will have to find another place. I want my office back. But with a moment of kind insight, I realize that their presence in my private space represents a sort of peace offering from her—she took them down for my sake, and she will, I think, for my sake not put them up again. She has made some small sacrifices to welcome me home. I am quite touched by this.

Yes, I will stay and wear the garments of this life. I will stay for Lora, because she will not let me go. If, having waited for me, she wants me back because, after everything, she loves me, what can I do except cling to her and fuck her good?

And yes, I will stay also because I am too timid (or too wise) to think I can find anything better for myself in another place. Even if I cannot forgive myself for it, I will stay. I do not say that this marriage—this life—is not a mistake, only that I have no choice.

For these are the people I—the word forces itself out—love. Eli and Ella, whom I raised from the time they were little and in whose gestures and jokes I recognize myself—after Hannah and Lora, who in the world is closer to me than they?

I hate them, I love them. I am the master of ambivalence.

Our bodies back in clothing, my wife and I held hands and chatted on the way to fetch our daughter once again from her non-sectarian community daycare group in the basement of the Athens Unitarian Church. "I'll wait out here," said Lora considerately at the church door. "Hannah's been waiting days for her Daddy to come for her."

So I passed alone through the dim marble vestibule.

Hannah didn't see me come in. I watched her for a moment, my one and only, playing with crayons and dolls. She seemed bigger to me, more competent, and I had a crazy, deep pang of missing her for the two months I had been gone. (Oh, I am full of feelings.) The caregiver, a fat and merry kindergarten teacher named Betsy, smiled and waved at me, then called to Hannah, "Hannah, your father is here." Hannah turned immediately and came toddle-racing toward me, yelling "Daddydaddydaddydaddy," and leapt without stopping into my outstretched arms. I twirled her around and bestowed three big kisses on her plump cheek, then hugged her to my chest.

"I am *glad* to see you, pumpkin," I tell her, smelling her soft skin, then beam at her while she pokes her fingers into my face and pulls at my beard, getting reacquainted. "I have stories to tell you and I have some gifts for you—"

"Oh, Daddydaddy," she suggests, "gimme."

The gifts are at home, I explain, but I have with me a candy bar that I tell her I will give to her toot-sweet, which she remembers means in a moment.

"I make a helfant," she says in her little voice, and she shimmies down from my arms and runs back to her table to bring me the scribble drawing she has made while thinking of an elephant. Kneeling beside her to look, I tell her how glad it makes me to be able to see her beautiful drawings once again. This is true; I have not felt so completely sincere in months.

I carry her and her drawing out to the marble lobby, where her stroller is parked against the wall. My heart is full of rejoicing. This at last is my uncomplicated homecoming.

About Hannah I have no doubts and no ambivalences. I am filled up with the sure knowledge that I would do anything for love of her. Her face, shaped and colored like mine, recognizably created through my influence, beams pure uncomplicated love back at me. Certain of my priorities, she has her own: "Canbar, Daddy," she coos and pats my hand with happy proprietorship as I strap her into her stroller. I pull out of my pocket and strip the wrapper off the Snickers bar I have carried since Ohio so she will have something sweet with which to remember my return, and we go out to Mommy, strings of chocolate drool already draped on Hannah's chin.

Hannah is thrilled to see her Mommy and Daddy together. I put my arm around Lora, making sure Hannah gets the message. Lora is not, I can tell, pleased that our plump Hannah is eating the candy bar she proudly holds up, but she does not say anything.

And so, a family tableau—husband and wife pushing child in a stroller—we proceed down a street in Athens, New York, going home.

Yes, I can enumerate many solid reasons for these years of blended-family confusion. Hasn't Mrs. Kramer framed them for us at other times? Lora and I did not have opportunity to get to know each other gradually *before* we had children, to test out our values and routines as just-the-two-of-us. Instead, from the first, we had the immediate needs of these children to deal with, needs exacerbated by the great loss they had suffered. And then we tried, so typically, to be an ordinary family, as if nothing had happened, as if we had no history of hurt to deal with. And then there were the constant stresses of the comings-and-goings of the children and their father; and their divided loyalties; and the financial obligations of a family of four.

And beyond all that, we had the difficulties of marriage itself. And those were made more intractable because we never planned our lives or discussed what we wanted or compared expectations, but had simply come together with the passionate faith that our love guaranteed our ambitions, sure that we would each get what we wanted but had never bothered to confess.

Some truths it doesn't help to know. Some facts are not sufficient to the task of explanation. Yet saying them, I force myself again to confront the inescapable: that this life, though not comfortable, fits me like a glove. In some terrible way, it is my true life.

Anyway, I cannot cast myself out into the historyless dark or break Hannah's soul in two with a divorce. In two weeks Eli and Ella will come back, and everything will begin to be again the way things are when they are here. I will survive, even if I do not change. Still uncertain of my place, I will applaud at my stepchildren's graduations and dance at their weddings. I will raise my own daughter and watch her become some combination of her mother and myself. I will write my poems. Life, wife and poetry are all one career in which I bruise my brain to find some meaning in the general run of the ordinary.

When I was a young boy, my mother, remembering her own past, which was mysterious to me, would sometimes weep in pain for something that could never be undone. I could not imagine then, as I first mounted the high horse of my own life's ambition, there could be a mistake that could not be undone. I surely did not believe that anything like that could ever happen to me—a grief like that could not be solaced, a disappointment that would remain like a thick stump forever, blocking other growth.

I put on the garments of my life. Nothing has changed, but Lora and I will start over. In this way, love, losing its passion, becomes a function of history—a fate instead of a choice.

I can live this life. It is better than most, in fact. I accept it.

Only a small pained voice intrudes:

No, this is not the heroic message that we set out in gladness to bear into the world when we began so long ago, is it, Cyna, my love?